USA TODAY and *Wall Street Journal* bestselling author **Janice Lynn** has a Master's in Nursing from Vanderbilt University and works as a nurse practitioner in a family practice. She lives in the southern United States with her Prince Charming, their children, their Maltese named Halo and a lot of unnamed dust bunnies that moved in after she started her writing career. Readers can visit Janice via her website at janicelynn.net.

Also by Janice Lynn

A Firefighter in Her Stocking
A Surgeon to Heal Her Heart
Heart Surgeon to Single Dad
Friend, Fling, Forever?
A Nurse to Tame the ER Doc
The Nurse's One Night to Forever
Weekend Fling with the Surgeon
Reunited with the Heart Surgeon

Discover more at millsandboon.co.uk.

THE SINGLE MUM HE CAN'T RESIST

JANICE LYNN

MILLS & BOON

First published in Great Britain 2023
by Mills & Boon, an imprint of HarperCollins*Publishers* Ltd,
1 London Bridge Street, London, SE1 9GF

www.harpercollins.co.uk

HarperCollins*Publishers*
Macken House, 39/40 Mayor Street Upper,
Dublin 1, D01 C9W8, Ireland

Large Print edition 2023

ISBN: 978-0-263-29733-1

07/23

FSC
www.fsc.org
MIX
Paper | Supporting
responsible forestry
FSC™ C007454

This book is produced from independently certified FSC™ paper
to ensure responsible forest management.
For more information visit: www.harpercollins.co.uk/green.

Printed and Bound in the UK using 100% Renewable Electricity
at CPI Group (UK) Ltd, Croydon, CR0 4YY

To Reesee.

Love you and am so proud of you.

CHAPTER ONE

"YOU'RE LOOKING AT him again."

While her best friend plopped down in a chair at the nurses' station, Nurse Jenny Robertson jerked her eyes away from where six feet of male physical perfection had gone into an Intensive Care Unit room at Chattanooga General Hospital.

"Don't be ridiculous." She tried not to sound too defensive at Laura's observation. Tristan Scott's dark, slightly wavy hair, sky-blue eyes and infectious smile did catch her eyes too often, but she wasn't acknowledging that to her bestie. "You just happened to look my way as I just happened to look up and he just happened to be there. That's all."

Roger Pennington's hazel eyes crinkled with amusement. "That's a lot of 'just happeneds.'"

"A whole lot." Laura's gaze shifted to where Tristan could be seen caring for his patient through the ICU's glass wall facing where they sat. A respiratory therapist, another nurse, and a tech were helping get his new admit settled. "But you and every other single woman who works here thinks our newest travel nurse is hot. Rightly so. If I hadn't felt the immediate sparks between you two, I'd be all over that scrumptiousness."

Roger snickered. Jenny rolled her eyes.

"If you think he's all that, go for it." Why had her stomach just twisted into a tight wad? Irked at herself, she lifted her chin. "You have my blessing to be 'all over that scrumptiousness.'"

"Your blessing?" Roger leaned against the rounded station desk that separated their workspace from their patients' rooms. "What is this, like 'olden days' girl code or something?"

Jenny pointed her finger at him. "You stay out of this."

Grinning, he held up his hands in mock defense. "Yes, ma'am."

"We've been friends since kindergarten," Laura reminded. "I know you better than anyone. Deny it all you want, but you like Tristan."

"If you know me so well, then you should know that, even if I did find him attractive and was willing to become involved, which I don't and

I'm not," she quickly added, "I'd never choose someone I work with."

"Otherwise, she wouldn't have been able to resist dating me."

Jenny and Laura snorted. Roger, who had dated the same woman since high school and was still completely infatuated with the ultrasonographer.

"You'd be a lonely man, Roger, if women got to choose who they were attracted to," Laura teased then turned her attention back to Jenny. "Admit it. Tristan gets you twitterpated."

"He's not my type." No one was her type. As in literally "no one." She didn't want a type or another man in her life. Some mistakes shouldn't be repeated. With few exceptions, she considered herself an intelligent person. Romantic involvements made up the bulk of her big life goofs.

Roger's face scrunched with exaggerated mortification. "Hot isn't your type? That seals the deal. You and I would never work."

Sighing, Jenny pushed away her tablet then swiveled her chair to face them.

"The man is a travel nurse," she pointed out, her tone clearly equating the label to the Bubonic plague. "He's here today, gone tomorrow. The last thing any of us needs is to get involved with someone who we know isn't staying."

"He'll be here three months."

Jenny gave Laura a "So what?" look.

"Three months is time for a whole lot of fun." Laura waggled her brows.

"Oh, yeah." Smirking, Roger gave her a high five.

Jenny shook her head at their antics. "I don't need that kind of fun."

"Girl, you need that kind of fun more than anyone I know," Laura insisted. "How long has it been? A year? Two? Three?"

Jenny's cheeks caught fire, or sure felt as if there were flames consuming them. Blazing infernos.

"It's not been nearly long enough that I've forgotten all the heartache that follows falling in love." She grabbed her tablet and tapped the screen a couple of times. Maybe if she looked busy, they'd leave her alone.

Roger's tone turned serious. "Please tell me you're not still hung up on he whose name we don't say? He never deserved you."

Did he mean Geoffrey or Carlos? Probably Geoffrey. He'd been her biggest heartbreak. Carlos had just been a brief reminder of why she was better off single.

"No, he didn't deserve me, but he taught me a valuable lesson that there are more important things in life than sex."

Like human decency and keeping promises you made to love and be true forever. People still did that, right?

"I wouldn't be opposed to a relationship with someone who believed in forever, someone who would always be there, but I've yet to meet someone with staying power. Besides, I don't miss sex," she continued. Who had time for sex? She sure didn't. Her life was full. "I'm abstinent by choice and content with that decision."

"Content is the wrong word choice when you're discussing your lack of a sex life." Laura's nose curled. "Girl, you need to have sex."

"I'm not sure what I missed, but I definitely missed something."

Flames engulfed Jenny's face, again. She'd missed Tristan coming out of his patient's room.

"Jenny was trying to convince me that sex isn't important." Laura filled him in, her dark eyes twinkling with merriment that he'd joined the conversation.

"Not if you aren't having sex with someone special," Jenny clarified, not sure why she felt the need to defend her stance.

Tristan's baby blues that had all the Intensive Care Unit agog studied Jenny. "Is there currently someone special in your life?"

Was he asking if she was having sex? It had been years. It was likely to be years before she had sex again, too. Or maybe she never would. She didn't mind. She'd liked sex okay, but it wasn't the be-all and end-all.

The way Tristan looked at her had her wondering if one night within those muscled arms would have her begging for more rather than feeling content to sleep alone night after night. Was that why he'd occupied so much of her thoughts since his arrival? Because her body instinctually recognized his in some Neanderthalian species-must-go-on way?

The timer she'd set on her phone beeped.

"There are a lot of special someones in my life," she assured with the smile she usually wore when her friends weren't harassing her about her love life—or lack thereof. "Currently, the special someone in Room Three needs my attention." With that, she rose to check on John

Rossberg. John was a sixty-two-year-old who'd been admitted with acute respiratory failure secondary to viral pneumonia. Putting on her personal protective equipment, she entered his room and exhaled with relief to have escaped the conversation.

Stepping up to his bedside, she silenced the beeping alarm.

"Good evening, Mr. Rossberg. This is Jenny. You're stuck with me again tonight," she told the unconscious man who had been her patient the evening before, as well. "As I told you when I came in after shift change, I was glad to hear you had a good day. Your white blood cell count has started coming down and your renal function is some better. Those are really good signs."

She liked talking to her patients, even the unconscious ones. Many of them were aware of at least bits and pieces of the world around them. She wanted to be a light in that dark world and often thought how lonely and scary it must be for a comatose patient to be aware of what was going on around them but unable to communicate.

"Your wife was here when I arrived tonight. She's a lovely woman and sure does love you.

She's gone home for the night, but said she'd be back first thing in the morning. Have I told you that you have excellent taste? She's such a sweetheart. She showed me photos of your grandchildren earlier this week. I told you about that, remember?"

She continued to chat while she changed out the empty intravenous fluid bag to a new one. "They are so cute and close in age to my four-year-old son, Sawyer. I know your family is anxious for you to get well so you can take your grandkids fishing. Your wife told me that was something special you do with them. Sawyer hasn't ever been fishing, but he adores the water and fish. We visited the aquarium and he absolutely loved it. I'm hoping to get him into swim lessons this summer. He's on a wait list at a facility near our home."

Once she had the bag updated, she rechecked his equipment. When finished, she lingered. Yes, she was avoiding going back to the nurses' station. Yes, if they were still there, her friends could see her and knew what she was doing. No, she wasn't ashamed to admit it. Not to herself.

"You don't mind my staying in here a bit longer, anyway, right?" she asked her patient, patting his hand. "You're much better company than my coworkers."

Especially her temporary coworker.

Tristan was bothersome. He had thrown her off-kilter the first night they'd met and every work night since. He was friendly, funny, helpful, and his smile reached his eyes. Jenny might not be interested, but she wasn't blind. Laura hadn't been wrong in calling him hot. He fit right in with their tight-knit ICU crew.

When she'd triple-checked Mr. Rossberg's vitals and told him all about the late spring Tennessee weather, she left the room, stripped off her protective gear and properly disposed of it, then sanitized. There wasn't anyone at the nurses' station when she got back there, but her reprieve didn't last long.

Tristan came out of the new admission's room and leaned against the edge of the desk.

"Everything okay with your patient?" he asked, giving her one of those smiles that reached his eyes, dug dimples into his cheeks, and had butterflies performing acrobatics in her belly.

Giving a polite-but-nothing-more smile, she nodded. "No new issues. I just needed to change his IV bag over and check his drips."

"Glad to hear it." He sounded sincere. Perhaps he was. He seemed to genuinely care about the patients. They'd had some excellent travel nurses on her unit, but the uncaring ones' lax attitude and frequent disappearing acts always irked. Their patients were people with loved ones. Their lives mattered and nothing with their care should be taken for granted.

Nodding, she went back to charting her encounter with Mr. Rossberg and hoped she didn't accidently insert the words *Tristan*, *scrumptious* or *great smile* anywhere into the record.

Tristan sat in the chair next to hers. "I'm sorry if I made you uncomfortable earlier."

"It wasn't your fault you walked up on Laura being Laura," she said without looking up.

"Still, I had no right to insert myself into a personal conversation. I'm sorry."

Ugh. Why did he have to be so nice? And so *hot*?

"No problem," she fibbed. Everything about him was problematic. His good manners, his dark, wavy hair that she longed to touch to see if it was as soft as it looked, his blue eyes that reminded her of the sky on the clearest of days, his frequent smile that reached those eyes and put an extra sparkle there, his… Ugh, yes, he was problematic. Monumentally so.

“Not that there’s anything wrong with your choice, but I can’t help but think that it’s a shame you aren’t interested in a relationship.”

Jenny’s breath caught. Was he making a general observation or implying personal disappointment?

“My choices aren’t any of your business.”

He gave a sheepish grin. “You’re right, and I need to apologize yet again for letting my curiosity get the better of me. Sorry.”

“Curiosity killed the cat,” she recited, keeping her tone flat so he wouldn’t mistake it for flirting.

He chuckled. “I’m no cat.”

Possibly not, but he was a man and probably tomcatted with the best of them. No matter how fluttery he made her insides, she needed to remember that.

She gave a tight smile, then focused her eyes on her tablet. But her mind was on the man watching her from where he hadn’t budged. Trying to ignore him, she tapped on her screen in the hope of finishing her charting.

“Have I done something to make you not like

me, Jenny? If so, I'd like to make that right." He cleared his throat, causing her eyes to open and her gaze to collide with his. "Actually, what I'd like is for us to be friends. Maybe after our shift ends, we could start over by my taking you to breakfast."

He wanted to take her to breakfast? To be friends? Jenny fought the urge to rub her temples. What was it about this night and people putting her on the spot?

There was something fragile in Jenny's big brown eyes; something that twisted Tristan's insides. From the moment they'd met, he'd wanted to know more about her and to erase the wariness that shone when their gazes met.

"There's a great place in the converted old warehouse building where the apartment I've rented is. It's not too far from the hospital."

"I figured you must live close as I've seen you bicycling to work."

"Cycling is great exercise and the complex really isn't that far away."

"Many of the older buildings that had sat empty for decades have found new life over the past few years. I'm glad."

Pleased that she hadn't immediately shut him down as he'd expected, Tristan nodded. "There are photos of the revitalization process hanging along the main floor's hallway. That floor is filled with shops, a workout facility, and a few restaurants. The upper floors are apartments. Mine's a small, furnished penthouse studio. The atmosphere is great. The food is even better."

She hesitated only a moment before doing as he'd expected.

"It sounds nice, but no thank you. As for the other—" fatigue etched itself onto her lovely face "—you've not done anything."

"Then you just don't like me?"

There was something off in the way she related to him compared with the other nurses, one of whom was also a travel nurse who had only started a week prior to Tristan. He'd seen her laughing with the guy on several occasions and had had to tamp down the jealous flash that had hit him at how easily she'd talked with him.

"I don't know you," she said defensively, sounding more flustered and shifting in her chair.

"And don't want to?" Part of him warned he should let it drop, but he might never get another opportunity to set the record straight. If there was something he could say, could do, that would put her at ease, that could have her smiling and laughing with him, then he'd jump through whatever hoops he needed to, to make that happen.

"You won't be here long," she observed, not meeting his eyes. "Whether or not we get to know each other is irrelevant."

Jenny didn't want a short-term relationship. He got that. He wasn't looking for a relationship, short or long, but from the moment he'd met her, he'd been intrigued.

"I'll be here for three months. That's long enough to make friends."

"That's long enough to make an acquaintance," she corrected. "Friendships take years."

She was wrong on that, too. He'd made many good friends during his life adventures. People he could call up and chat with or go months, years even, in between seeing without awkward feelings when they reconnected.

"You don't believe two people can meet and instantly know if they connect as friends?"

She harrumphed. "Friends at first sight?"

"Yes."

Her expression was doubtful. “And you thought this about me when we met? That we would be friends at first sight?”

“I’d hoped we would be friends. That’s what I thought when we first met, that you were someone I wanted to be friends with. I still want that.”

He couldn’t recall having ever met someone he’d so instantly wanted to know. Jenny had been smiling at something someone had said and Tristan had been instantly hooked, wanting to see her smile again, only with him being the cause of her happiness. When she’d turned and her big brown eyes had collided with his, visions of kissing her full lips had hit him so hard he’d mentally doused cold water over his thoughts to prevent what could have been an embarrassing situation.

How he’d reacted had caught him off guard. Her standoffish reaction even more so because he’d swear that he’d seen mutual attraction in that initial moment. Whatever he’d seen, she’d masked her emotions, smiled her way through introductions, and high-tailed it into a patient’s room, avoiding him the rest of the night.

“Other than Laura, I don’t fraternize with my coworkers outside the hospital, and Laura doesn't count since we've been best friends since elementary school." Jenny's expression became thoughtful. "I don't spend a lot of time with Laura away from work these days, either." She shot a tight smile. "You'll understand why based upon the conversation you walked in on."

Leaning back in the chair, he crossed his arms. "How long have you worked at Chattanooga General?"

Frowning at his question, she hesitated then said, "Four years."

"That makes you what? About twenty-six or twenty-seven?"

"Twenty-five," she corrected.

"This was your first job after graduation?"

Eyes narrowed, she nodded.

"Did you do a clinical rotation at this hospital?"

"No, I did clinicals at Erlanger, which was a wonderful experience, and then my last rotation was in Ringgold." Her face pinched, making him wonder if that experience hadn't been so wonderful. "Laura convinced me to apply here as it's where she'd done her clinical rotations and she loved it. She knew I had no plans to apply in Ringgold." Perhaps realizing she'd revealed too much, her expression darkened. "I'm glad I did, as we both landed in the ICU."

Tristan suspected knowing what had happened in Ringgold would reveal a lot about Jenny and why she had so many walls. Probably a man she'd met there, but who knew? He'd bite his tongue rather than ask when he knew it would shut down their current conversation.

"Are you originally from Chattanooga?"

She nodded. "Not far from here."

"Did you always want to be a nurse?" he rushed on, wanting to get her beyond where her thoughts had gone, in the hope she wouldn't take off on some pretend nursing mission when all was currently calm on the unit.

"My mom is a nurse. I've always admired how she took care of people." Jenny's tone softened. "She's the best, so kind and gentle with those in her care. It makes sense that I want to be as much like her as I can."

The love and admiration she felt laced her words and Tristan felt a twist of envy. How great it must be to be so proud of your parents?

"Well, she raised you right, or maybe it's just good caregiver genetics, because you're a great nurse, Jenny."

Her cheeks pinkened. "I— Thank you, but you've only been here a couple of weeks, so you might want to save that observation for a few months from now."

"I knew you were a wonderful nurse after the first night I worked with you."

Filled with curiosity, her eyes met his. "How can you be so sure?"

"You're efficient. Constantly on task to make sure your patients get great care. Smart. Compassionate. And your coworkers love you, as do your patients. How much they do says a lot."

"Most of my patients are unconscious, so there's that."

He laughed. "True, but they love you when they wake up and see the kindness on your face that matches the kindness in your voice when you're talking to them even when you're not sure they hear you."

"How do you know I talk to my patients?"

"There are glass walls separating the rooms from the hallway," he pointed out, grinning as he told her the obvious. "I've seen you talking to your patients. You're constantly chatting away, even to the unconscious ones. Your face gets so animated at times that I wonder what you could possibly be saying to them with such enthusiasm."

"You've met my best friend. It's quite possible that I chat with unconscious people as a reaction to her." Jenny's lips twitched. "Besides, for all you know, I could be telling them to get off their tushes so I can give their bed to someone else or so I could have an easy go for the rest of my shift."

"I'm going with my gut on this one. You're a good nurse. The compassionate kind I hope I'd get if I were ever in an intensive care unit."

Her cheeks pinkened again. They did that a lot, the splash of color contrasting with her fair skin. Dark hair, dark eyes, porcelain skin that brightened at the lightest comment.

"Let's hope you never are." She bit into her lower lip. "Is there something you're wanting, Tristan? Because a game of Twenty Questions and flattery will not win points with me."

Was that what she thought he was trying to do? Flatter her? For that matter, what was he trying to do? He liked his life uncomplicated. Jenny was complicated. He might not know a lot about her, but he was positive she made Riemann's hypothesis seem as nothing more than simple mathematics.

"I want to be your friend." *More than that*, an inner voice whispered. He had never dated co-workers during his short stints, not even ones who knew the score and were as footloose and fancy-free as he was. Jenny wanted someone who was going to stick around. And yet, he admitted that if she crooked her finger, that rule would be tossed to the wind.

"You'll have to settle for being my temporary coworker," she said without a smile or finger crook. "I'm not in the market for new friends."

CHAPTER TWO

THE FOLLOWING NIGHT, Jenny managed to avoid being alone with Tristan. Knowing her friends were watching, she'd even managed to act semi-normal around him while under their eagle eyes. The night had been uneventful to where just past midnight they'd finished their charts, had recently assessed their patients, and were sitting at the nurses' station. The group had been giving recommendations on local spots for Tristan to visit.

"Have you checked out the Ocoee or the Nantahala?" Roger asked when Tristan mentioned he'd worked a couple of summers as a white-water rafting guide. "They're great for kayaking or rafting, although probably not as challenging as what you did in Colorado."

"I've not, but a rafting trip is on my Chattanooga to-do list. I've been curious about the Ocoee. I'd seen it's only about an hour. I've not looked into the Nantahala as it's further away. Which river do you recommend?"

Roger smiled. "Lucia and I have done each one a few times. The Ocoee has higher-graded rapids and is closer, but the Nantahala is great, too."

"I've done trips down both, too," Crystal, the charge nurse, said. "Roger's right. They're so much fun. I've not been in years."

"I've been once, but it was years ago, too, with a church youth group," Laura said, glancing toward Jenny. "Do you remember that? Your mom had gallbladder surgery and you didn't get to go."

Jenny nodded. At the time, she'd been sad, but she hadn't been able to leave her mother at home alone. She'd always choose family over fun.

"We should put a trip together," Laura suggested, her eyes bright with excitement. "We can go up on a weekend we have off, camp, raft, and have a great time. Doesn't that sound like fun, Jenny? You'd finally get to go down the river."

"I don't feel as if I've missed out, Laura. Sixteen-year-old me may have wanted to go, but adult Jenny has better things to do. White-water rafting isn't my thing."

"What is your thing?"

All eyes went to Tristan, including Jenny's. "Not much. Work, sleep, eat, spend time with family. I'm completely boring."

"I find that difficult to believe."

Her coworkers' gazes bounced back and forth between her and Tristan. Jenny fought a sigh. Why were they looking at them as if they were the evening's entertainment?

"Regardless of what you believe, it's true." She didn't see boring as a problem given it meant nothing unexpected ever happened. Boring was good.

"Don't listen to her." Laura spoke up. "She's cautious not boring."

Jenny glared at her friend.

"I work at a hospital. I see what happens when people aren't cautious. There's no reason to take unnecessary chances." As Sawyer's mother, she had to be cautious. How could she not be when he depended upon her?

Tristan's brow arched. "You never take unnecessary chances?"

"Life has taught me that being cautious is in my own best self-interest. I get hurt when I'm not cautious."

Jenny had revealed far too much. But since

Tristan had asked and the others were all waiting for her response, so be it.

"Caution isn't always a good thing, Jenny," Tristan countered earnestly. "The world would quit advancing if no one took chances. Just think of the medical field alone if no one had ever tried something different."

The conversation was cut short by two patient alarms sounding almost simultaneously, one of which was Mr. Rossberg's and the other was a patient of Roger's. They jumped up simultaneously.

"Sorry, not sorry, I've got to go." Grateful to leave the conversation, Jenny stopped only long enough to put on protective gear before entering the ICU room.

Even with his volume-controlled ventilator system and supplemental oxygen, John Rossberg's blood oxygen saturation level was dipping into the low- to mid-eighties. His baseline oxygen had been running in the upper eighties to low nineties since his admission. The PIP—peak inspiratory pressure—had elevated to just above thirty, meaning it was taking more work by the machine to achieve a set ebb-and-flow inhalation pressure. Thus, the triggered alarm. The PIP level wasn't so high, however, that Jenny immediately thought pneumothorax, but she couldn't rule out that he didn't have a collapsed lung or even pulmonary edema.

Quickly, she did a visual assessment, noting the symmetric rise and fall of his chest while she checked his pulse oximeter, making sure it had a good connection. Convinced it did, she checked his endotracheal tube, making sure his bite block was doing its job to prevent him from biting into the tube and that his lip line location was still good. Both were perfectly in place.

Listening to his chest, she detected air movement throughout his lung fields in sync with the ventilator breathing for her patient. She also heard crackles that shouldn't be there.

"Okay, Mr. Rossberg, what's going on here?" she asked, checking his extremities for swelling that might indicate fluid overload. His compression hoses were working, there were no noticeable changes in the size of his legs or arms. He was being fed via a nasogastric tube and the markings on the NG tube were still where they should be, so he likely hadn't aspirated from a feeding. But it wasn't impossible.

"You aren't trying to build up fluid in your

lungs, are you? You know that doesn't make this nurse happy, right? No worries, though. I'm going to contact your doctor to let him know what's going on, get a portable X-ray ordered, along with anything else he wants done, and then I'll suction the mucus to hopefully help you get rid of whatever is causing those extra lung sounds and increased peak inspiratory pressures. We'll have your lungs clear soon."

Or at least clear out as much of the sputum as she could to where it wasn't interfering so much with his oxygen saturation and lung pressure. With the respiratory failure that had sent him into multi-organ breakdown, he was so fragile and at risk for complications.

"I can't have you getting pneumonia." She continued talking to him despite nothing on his monitors changing in response to her doing so. He probably didn't know she was there. Maybe, under the circumstances, that was better, because she didn't want him sensing how concerned she was at the changes in his vitals readings.

"Need help?" Tristan asked, coming into the room. With the mask covering the lower half of his face, the blue of his eyes popped even more. "I knew from the last time we were in here that it was about time to turn him, so I thought I'd see if you needed help with that or anything else."

As much as she'd rather it be someone other than Tristan, she'd take what help she could get. Turning Mr. Rossberg with all his lines was a two-plus person job. "His oxygen saturation has decreased, his PIP is above thirty, and he has crackles in his lower lobes bilat. If you'll get suction started, I'll call Dr. Willis. He'll want to get a portable chest X-ray ordered and repeat labs at the minimal."

"Sure thing." He set about inserting a suction tip into Mr. Rossberg's endotracheal tube as Jenny called the intensivist.

"Dr. Willis said to order the X-ray and bloodwork," she said when she'd hung up her phone. "I'll put the orders in so Radiology and the lab can get someone up here."

Entering the orders into the electronic medical system, Jenny glanced to where Tristan was suctioning her patient, noting the rusty-colored sputum he was removing from Mr. Rossberg's lungs.

Perhaps having sensed that she was looking his way, Tristan asked, "Pneumococcal pneumonia?"

"Maybe. His original PCR test showed viral with no bacterial. As much as I hate to think he's picked up a nosocomial bacterial infection while here, it's possible." She sighed, her mask causing the warm air to fan the portions of her face beneath the material. "His white blood cell counts were normal earlier today and were decreased at time of his admission."

"Which is consistent with viral." Glancing at the rusty sputum again, Tristan's gaze then met hers. "You think he's bleeding?"

In Mr. Rossberg's condition, with the endotracheal tube, it was possible that he'd suffered an injury in placement or that the tube had irritated already fragile tissue.

"I doubt it. His sputum isn't bright red, so, if it's blood, it's old and mixed with mucus." She shrugged. "If a bleed, we'll know soon enough." She hoped that wasn't it. She wasn't sure Mr. Rossberg could survive surgical repair of a bleed if it came to needing that. "We'll get a culture and a new PCR test sent off."

"Right," Tristan agreed as Jenny finished adding the orders for another polymerase chain reaction test.

"Given his current status, it isn't the priority,

but I'll need to turn him to a Semi-Fowler position after his chest imaging." While the staff rotated his on-side positions every couple of hours to help prevent bedsores, she knew that given his current condition, the on-his-back bed angle would better facilitate his lung expansion and ventilation. "We'll need at least one other person in here to help make sure his lines stay in place."

"Laura is helping Roger with one of his patients. That's why you got stuck with my help, but they may be finished by the time the radiology technologist gets the bedside chest view pictures."

Jenny nodded. "If so, we can call for Crystal, or if she's busy then one of the respiratory therapists can assist. I've entered another consult at Dr. Willis's request. You want me to take over the suctioning or to draw his labs?"

"Get the labs and I'll finish up this."

In silence they worked together, taking a short step-back break as the X-ray technician took her shots.

"Looks like fluid build-up bilateral, worse on the right," the tech said. "I'll get these off to the radiologist for an official reading and have him message Dr. Willis."

Once Mr. Rossberg's pressures and sats were somewhat improved, although not back to his baseline, Jenny, Tristan, Crystal and a male respiratory therapist painstakingly repositioned him.

Jenny and Tristan worked on one side. Crystal and Blake worked on the other, taking extreme care as, inch by inch they moved him onto his back. Twice during the move, Jenny brushed against Tristan. Twice she had a blink of awareness of how close he was, how easy to work with, and how very virile.

The man gave off so many pheromones that even in this crazy moment her body couldn't not react. Stupid primal instincts. Mother Nature had a wicked sense of humor.

When they finished, Crystal and Blake left the room. Wanting to stay close until she was assured Mr. Rossberg's vitals were going to remain stable, Jenny remained near her patient's bed, as did Tristan.

"Even if only minimally improved, he seems stable at the moment, so I'm off to check on my patient," Tristan told her, standing next to where she watched the rise and fall of Mr. Rossberg's chest. "Anything I can help with before I go?"

Grateful no monitors displayed how her heart rhythm sped up at his nearness, Jenny shook her head. “I appreciate your help. Thank you. I’ll be in here awhile as I want to be close in case anything changes, but if you need help repositioning your patient, buzz me.”

Although his mask blocked the lower half of his face, his eyes crinkled, letting her know he was smiling. “No problem. I was glad to help. I enjoy working with you, Jenny.”

She felt the same. Unfortunately.

Later that night, Jenny leaned against the break-room counter, eyes closed, waiting for the toaster oven to finish heating her early a.m. “lunch.” John Rossberg had remained stable, with no evidence of active bleeding, a pneumothorax, or a pulmonary embolism. Though his white blood cell count had significantly spiked, his differentials indicated that he had developed a secondary infection. Dr. Willis had prescribed a strong antibiotic as a precaution while they awaited his test results.

“You okay?”

Jenny sighed. Like a bad penny, Tristan kept showing up. Did he purposely seek her out? *Why ask what you already know?* He did. Part of her was flattered and another frustrated as not being near him would be easier.

"It's after four in the morning, so I'm a little tired, but otherwise, I'm fine."

"Yep. Tonight's flown by."

She was glad he thought so. For the most part, she felt as if it had dragged.

"You sure you're okay? You're rubbing your neck," he pointed out.

Jenny's hand fell. She hadn't noticed.

"I was concerned that you might have injured yourself when we turned Mr. Rossberg—he's a good two hundred pounds—or perhaps when you were helping with Mattie."

She shook her head. "Like I said, I'm fine. Just a little tired. How is Mattie?"

His new admit from the night before had come to the floor in multiple organ failure after the young woman had overdosed on a benzodiazepine prescription.

"Alive, still. Barely." He exhaled a long breath. "I always find taking care of overdose patients difficult."

"Really?" The toaster oven beeped. Jenny pulled her food from it, testing to make sure it was warm throughout, then breathed in the delicious aroma of her mother's chicken casserole. Geneva loved cooking and, by and large, Jenny let her reign in their kitchen. "That surprises me, because we see some icky stuff."

"It's more that most of our patients are battling something they didn't have much direct control over. With an overdose patient—" he shrugged "—I can't help but think that they should be out living life and not fighting for every breath in an ICU."

"There are those who would argue that an addict doesn't have much direct control over their choices, either," Jenny observed, her tone soft as part of her understood, agreed even, with what he was saying.

"You're right," he admitted. "I should keep that in mind. It just seems such a waste of a precious life."

He wasn't wrong.

"I doubt any of our overdose patients woke up one day and thought 'I want to be an addict.'"

"Most don't mean to overdose, either," he agreed. "But far too many end up with something laced with bad stuff or they accidentally take too much."

Jenny nodded. "I struggle the most with the ones who intentionally take too much or self-harm. Did you bring something to eat? I have way too much chicken casserole and am willing to share."

Now why had she just offered to give him some of her food? That was something a friend would do and she'd already pointed out that they weren't going to be friends.

"That smells wonderful and it is tempting." He opened the fridge and pulled out a drink bottle. "But I typically just drink a protein shake while at work."

She wrinkled her nose. "For your entire twelve-plus-hours shift? How do you survive?"

Although grabbing a bite was almost impossible some nights, Jenny never willingly skipped her meal break.

He grinned. "No need to worry. I'm not wasting away."

Jenny couldn't prevent her glance from roaming over his broad shoulders and thick chest that tapered at his waist. She swallowed the lump in her throat. Yeah, he definitely wasn't wasting away.

"I eat a big meal before coming to work," he

continued. "While working, I find I do best if I don't eat a lot, just drink plenty of water and protein."

"That seems to be working well for you." Duh! Why had she said such a stupid thing?

His eyes sparkled. "I'm glad you think so."

Yeah, she'd stepped right into that one. Rather than respond, she took a bite of her casserole. A small bite as she sure didn't want to risk choking and him thinking she'd purposely set up his having to save her.

"Laura tells me that you two went to school together your entire lives, including nursing school."

Jenny was grateful for the subject change. "Yes, we attended University of Tennessee together after graduating high school."

"In Knoxville?"

"Chattanooga," she corrected. "University of Tennessee has five campuses, including Knoxville and Memphis."

"That's right. Was Roger in your class, too?"

"I didn't meet him until I came to work here after…" Jenny paused. She did not want to discuss Geoffrey with Tristan. "After nursing school graduation," she finished, hoping he bought her cover.

Tristan's eyes darkened just enough that she knew he'd picked up that she hadn't said what she'd almost originally intended to. Rather than prompt her for more information, he said, "Laura's a good one."

"You won't hear any arguments from me." Well, except when it came to Tristan himself and Laura's teasing about his extremely warm temperature. Being around Tristan really was like being in a torrent heat wave. *Hot. Hot. Hot.* Resisting the urge to fan her face, she said, "She's my best friend."

Tristan's patient pager went off. "Hmm, none of Mattie's lines should need changing. I checked them right before coming in here to grab my drink."

Popping the top back onto her meal prep container and shoving it into the fridge, she offered, "I'll go with you in case you need an extra set of hands."

Already heading toward the door, he smiled. "Thanks."

"No problem. Good patient care is always my top priority."

That was the only reason she'd offered to help.

* * *

"Good morning," Jenny greeted the four-year-old sitting at the kitchen bar and munching on his cereal a few exhausting hours later. She kissed the top of his tawny head, loving the fresh smell of his shampoo, then walked over to the woman stirring a teaspoon of sugar into a "Volunteer" coffee mug. "Morning, Mom. Did you have a good night?"

"Every night spent with my grandson is a good night," her mom assured her, handing over the coffee. "Just as every night with you was a good night when you were growing up. Still is, actually."

"Love you, too." Jenny took a sip, savoring the hot decaffeinated liquid hitting her throat. She preferred caffeinated, but never indulged when she had to be asleep in less than an hour. Her rest schedule was on a tight timeline. She didn't do anything that might throw it off kilter. "Mmm...that's good. Thank you." Her gaze met her mother's. "For everything."

Gratitude was mild for what she felt. She'd have found a way when she'd gotten pregnant during nursing school, but having the support of the best woman she'd ever known and having her to stay with Sawyer on the nights Jenny couldn't be home had made finishing school and going to work so much easier. When Jenny worked weeknights, the day shift replacement charge nurse came in a few minutes early for the report so Jenny could skedaddle as quickly after shift change as possible. It wasn't much time but being there as a part of her son's mornings…well, she hoped someday he'd realize how important it was to her, how much she wanted to be there for him, and to be a part of his life.

"You're welcome, honey." Geneva smiled. "I put the lunch you had prepacked into his school bag and started a load of towels in the washer that you'll want to change over when you get back from dropping him off at school."

Her mother had offered to drop him off on her way to the assisted living where she worked an eight-to-five shift, but Jenny had always refused. She prized the precious time spent with Sawyer each morning and seeing his smile when, after she'd walked him into his preschool, he'd turn and wave.

"Mom, did you know that Grandma likes frogs?" Sawyer asked seemingly out of the blue in between bites of his breakfast.

"She does?" Suppressing a smile, Jenny's eyes went to her mother's.

Sawyer's soft, curl-covered head bobbed up and down. "We watched a show about frogs last night, and she helped me look them up online so we could learn more." His eyes lit with excitement. "Grandma liked that."

Jenny's mother smiled indulgently. "What can I say? He's broadening my horizons one amphibian at a time. We searched for the frog species you kiss to transform into a Prince Charming, but never came across that breed."

"You want to kiss a frog? I thought you liked Giles."

"I do like Giles. The frog was for you."

Jenny groaned. "The only frog I'm kissing is sitting in this chair. Let's see if he turns into a prince." She placed a noisy kiss on Sawyer's cheek then pulled back to stare at him. "Nope, not a prince yet. Maybe it takes a bunch of kisses."

She began kissing his cheeks over and over, triggering giggling protests.

"Stop. Stop. I'm not a frog."

Jenny paused in her sloppy cheek kisses to inspect him. "You sure about that?"

He nodded his head. "Grandma wants to find a big frog for you so you can be a princess like in the fairy tales."

Jenny snorted, glancing toward her mother. "She does, does she? You'll have to remind her that amphibians can be royal pains and I'm quite content with my life as it is."

Content. There was that word again. Because she was content, that's why it had popped up again. Why did others not seem to believe that?

By the time Jenny got back home after her preschool run, changed the washed towels over to the dryer, showered and climbed into bed, she'd get about six hours of sleep before going to pick Sawyer up from school. It wasn't a lot, but it would suffice.

Yawning, she set her alarm then rolled over, expecting to go to sleep as she usually passed out when her head hit the pillow. Instead, Tristan's face popped into her head. His handsome, smiling face.

"Ribbit."

Oh, no, he hadn't just said that! Tristan was not a frog who would magically morph into Prince Charming from a kiss. He was a travel nurse who would kiss today and be gone tomorrow.

She squeezed her eyes tightly shut as if that would somehow make him disappear from her mind.

"Ribbit. Ribbit. Ribbit."

Seriously, if the man wanted to be her friend then he'd best just shut the croak up and stay out of her head. She didn't need his interfering with her sleep.

Only, for the longest time, she couldn't stop the thoughts of him, of his smile, of his easygoing nature, of his "hotness." When she finally slept, she dreamt he really was a frog, complete with a lopsided crown sitting on his handsome head.

CHAPTER THREE

"NEED HELP?"

Jenny did, but she'd been looking for Roger, not this man, smiling so big she feared she might fall right into his dimples. She was more than a little irritated with him, through no real fault of his own. But short of lifting Mr. Rossberg by herself, yes, she needed his help.

Because of him, she'd barely slept and when she had, he had played a lead role in her dreams.

Dreams? Ha, more like an X-rated movie that had started out with a frog-morphing-into-a-prince kiss. She'd awakened breathless and achy.

Her eyes dropped to his mouth. His very talented, kissable mouth that had done amazing things to her.

No! His mouth wasn't talented and had never been anywhere near her lips, her neck, or anywhere else. Of course, he'd been phenomenal because it hadn't been real. He probably had bad breath or a saliva disorder or some other warty ailment that would turn her off. No one was as perfect as he seemed. Not even in fairy tales.

"Yes, your help would be great." Not really, but her patient came first. At home…well, at home, he wasn't welcome. Hopefully, today was a one-off because of Laura and Roger's crazy conversation, those innocent brushings against each other when they'd been repositioning Mr. Rossberg last night, and the odd kissing-a-frog conversation with Sawyer and her mother.

"You look tired. Did you not get much sleep today?" Tristan eyed her as he slipped his arms through his protective gown.

She frowned, trying to determine if he was concerned or if he somehow knew that it was his fault she'd not gotten her usual six hours of shut-eye between dropping off and picking up Sawyer.

"Is that your way of saying I look bad?" she asked, trying to focus on the negative where he was concerned rather than on how her heart was tapping a funny rhythm at his closeness. Not a normal *lub-dub, lub-dub* beat, but a wacky *rib-bit, rib-bit.* What was wrong with her?

"I didn't say you looked bad. I said you looked

tired. There's a difference." His eyes were full of appreciation. "I doubt you ever look bad."

She harrumphed. "I've already pointed out that flattery will go nowhere with me."

"I'm not trying to flatter you, Jenny." He sounded sincere. "Just pointing out the truth."

"Yeah, well, you've never seen me fresh out of bed." Her words spilled forth naturally, without thought. The second they did, she cringed at how he could interpret them. At how she interpreted them, possibly because in her dreams he had seen her fresh out of bed just a few hours ago.

"You don't wear much makeup, so it's hard to imagine that you'd look that different, but you know best, so if you say so..." Then he surprised her by grinning. "For whatever it's worth, I even understand. It takes me hours to achieve all this."

Biting into her lower lip, she tried to determine if he was teasing. The twinkle in his eyes said he was, and he'd never come across as vain, more unaware of how truly attractive he was, if anything.

"I'd hate to see you not trying if that—" snarling her nose, she gave him an up-and-down look "—takes hours."

Had that been her teasing back? No. No. No. She needed to keep her guard up, remain professional, not playful.

"You're right. You shouldn't see that." He smiled then gestured to her patient's room. "Any sign of regaining consciousness?"

Jenny shook her head. "I keep hoping I'll get to work and hear that he woke up, but nothing so far. His pneumonia doesn't seem to be clearing."

"It's never easy when our patients don't get well, is it?"

Jenny paused in donning her protective equipment to stare at him. She wasn't sure why, but she hadn't expected the deep compassion in his voice.

"No, but Mr. Rossberg is going to get better. I refuse to let him not."

Tristan's eyes smiled above his mask. "I stand by my initial assessment."

"What's that?" she asked, stepping into Mr. Rossberg's room.

"That you're a great nurse. Your mother must be so proud to know you followed in her footsteps and take such good care of your patients."

Warmth spread through her at his compliment. "I— Thank you."

"Better be careful, Jenny, because if I didn't know better, I'd think my flattery just worked a little with you." His tone was soft, teasing, as they made their way over to Mr. Rossberg's hospital bed.

"You keep thinking that if you like, but I'll know better, Kermit."

His forehead furrowed. "Who?"

Fighting a smile, and a bit of horror at what she'd called him, Jenny shook her head then touched her patient's arm. "Mr. Rossberg, it's Jenny. I'm here with another nurse, Tristan. He's helped with your care before, remember? He's going to assist while I suction some of the secretions built up in your lungs, so you get better air exchange, isn't that great? We're going to have you breathing easier soon so you can go fishing with that adorable grandson of yours."

"We're having a team-building event next weekend," Roger announced, dropping into the chair next to Jenny's at the nurses' station. "Your presence is required."

First tapping Save, Jenny glanced up from her charting. "What kind of event?"

"White-water rafting." Roger's voice filled

with excitement. "After our conversation about it, we decided to put together a trip with Tristan."

Jenny's stomach twisted.

"Perhaps you'll also recall from that conversation, that I'm not interested in white-water rafting."

Or in spending time with Tristan outside of work.

"Come on, Jenny. At least hear me out," Roger insisted. "Like what Laura suggested, we're driving to the Ocoee, camping on Friday night, rafting on Saturday, camping again that night, then driving back on Sunday, sleeping all day, then working all Sunday night."

He made it sound so simple, but Jenny shook her head.

"You forget that I'm not free to just take off for a weekend camping trip on the spur of the moment." Nor did she want to. She cherished her weekends with Sawyer when she was not scheduled to work. There was always lots to be done around the house, but she let him pick an activity for them to do together. She never knew if he was going to want to make cookies or go to the park or play board games. Sawyer's pick was as spur-of-the-moment as she got these days.

"Couldn't your mom watch Sawyer so that you could go with us?" Laura asked as she joined them. That her friend immediately knew what they'd been discussing said they'd been talking about it just prior to Roger returning to the nurses' station. "Not that I don't love hanging with Sawyer," Laura continued, "but it would be so good to spend time together away from work. It's been forever since you and I did that."

Guilt hit that they only spent time together at work or when Laura joined her and Sawyer. Did that make her a bad friend?

"I hate to ask when she already does so much." Not that her mother wouldn't jump all over sending Jenny if she thought there might be a few frogs around. That had her dream popping back into her head. Yeah, the last thing she needed was a camping trip with Tristan around. "Y'all go. Have fun. White-water rafting really isn't my thing."

"How do you know?" Roger asked.

Jenny blinked. "What do you mean how do I know? I just do."

"Have you ever been white-water rafting?"

She shook her head. "You know I haven't because Laura mentioned the missed church trip."

"You might enjoy rafting," he offered.

"I might not and then I'd be stuck in a flimsy raft floating down a raging river."

"Not that raging," Roger corrected.

"Says the guy who plans to jump out of an airplane to celebrate his thirtieth birthday this fall," Jenny quipped.

"You should do that with me." At her horrified look, Roger grinned. "Fine. No sky-diving for our Jenny, but at least say you'll think about going on the rafting trip."

"Besides the obvious reasons for my not going on y'all's impromptu trip, I don't own the first piece of camping equipment."

"You don't need anything," Laura declared. "I've got an extra sleeping bag and you can stay in my tent with me. I'll pack double, right down to bringing extra water shoes, so no excuses. It'll be like a sleepover. All you need to do is say yes."

The yearning in Laura's voice got to Jenny, but she wasn't asking her mother to keep Sawyer, not when doing so put herself in danger. She didn't mean the rafting part, either. Being around Tristan threatened her far more than taking on the river.

"I appreciate the invite, but I'm a mom first. My weekend off work is my time with Sawyer. As much as I adore y'all, I'm not giving that up to go rafting."

"Giles's grandson will be visiting with him this weekend."

Propping her cell phone between her shoulder and her ear, Jenny watched the timer count down on the toaster oven warming her work "lunch." She'd been running nonstop since arriving earlier that evening and was glad things had settled down early enough for her to make a call to tell Sawyer good-night and to chat with her mother afterward. That her mother's voice rang with happiness had Jenny smiling. Her mother had been dating the widower who worked at the assisted-living home with her for about a year and they'd been hinting about marriage. Jenny liked Giles, but even more, she liked how her mother lit up when she talked about him.

"He's bringing Eli to the aquarium in Gatlinburg on Friday night. There's a sleepover event with church," her mother continued, her voice breathy. "Giles invited Sawyer and me to go with them. Please say yes."

Her mother wanted Sawyer to do a church sleepover on the same weekend as the rafting trip? Had Laura called her mother and arranged this?

"I'm sure he'd have a great time." They'd visited the Chattanooga aquarium but had never been to the one in east Tennessee, much less slept over. No doubt Sawyer would love an overnight excursion. "When a group books an event, they sleep under the shark tank there, don't they? He'd be so excited that he might not sleep a wink."

"That's what Giles said—that we would be sleeping under the sharks. I'm not sure how I feel about that," her mother said with a low laugh, "but I know Sawyer would love it. We thought we'd spend the weekend in Gatlinburg and do some things with the boys, maybe minigolf or go to Parrot Mountain."

Jenny's stomach twisted. Other than when she was at work, her son had never spent a night away from her. "You want Sawyer to spend the whole weekend with you and Giles in Gatlinburg?"

"We'd watch him closely," her mother promised, blasting Jenny with guilt. Her mother loved Sawyer and wanted to have this fun trip with him.

"Oh, Mom, you know I trust you completely with Sawyer. It's not that, it's just...you already do so much, and for the whole weekend? Are you sure you want to take that on, too?"

"Absolutely. This would be such a fun weekend for us. I really do love spending time with him."

"Sawyer or Giles?" she teased, taking her dish from the toaster oven and testing the temperature.

Her mother's laugh said it all. "Giles is a good man, Jenny. I really think he might be the one."

The knot in her belly tightened. Not that she didn't want her mother happy, but mostly, she didn't want her hurt.

"I'm happy for you, Mom." She really was. Jenny's father had left before she'd been born. She only recalled a few men in her mother's life. A very few, and none of them had stuck around for long. Based on the one breakup conversation she'd accidentally overheard, she was to blame for that. Her split with Carlos had pretty much been an echo of that. Some men didn't want to be seriously involved with a woman who was a package deal.

"Now, how about you spend this weekend finding that Prince Charming frog to make you happy?"

Jenny snorted. She should have known their conversation would eventually turn to her finding a man. Everyone seemed to think she needed one.

"I am happy, Mom. No frog, or Prince Charming, required." She spoke the truth. She was happy. She had a good job, a home, her mom and Sawyer. Plus, her mother's homemade lasagna, she thought, taking a bite of the spicy pasta. Mmm… Life was good.

"That's not really what I meant. Of course, you're happy. But wouldn't it be wonderful to have someone to share that happiness with? You're a beautiful young woman, Jenny. I don't want you going through life alone the way I did."

"I think you're biased, Mom, but I appreciate how you see and love me." Jenny took a deep breath. "I'm also glad you've met someone who has given you so much happiness. I like Giles a lot. But that doesn't mean I want that, too. I have you and Sawyer. I'm content."

Content. Why did that word keep popping up

and seem to be a negative? Content was good, right?

"I worry about you, Jenny. I can't bear the thought of you sitting at home alone. Come with us."

For a moment, Jenny considered doing just that but then thought better of it. Her mother would be throwing every single male on the trip her way. No thank you.

"Promise me that you won't volunteer to work at the hospital."

"Volunteering at the hospital is a good thing. The extra money would come in handy to do some things around the house I've been wanting to update. Plus, I want to get that playground for Sawyer's birthday. Volunteering to work is exactly what I should do."

"You're going to work all weekend, aren't you? If he was here, you'd take the time to play rather than work." Her mother sighed, sounding as if she was considering canceling her own plans.

Jenny didn't want that. As much as the time away from her son was going to have her missing him, Sawyer would enjoy it.

"Actually, I got invited on a camping trip to the Ocoee with Laura and some of our work friends.

I hadn't thought to go, but since Sawyer will be with you, I think I might."

What was she saying?

"Seriously?" Her mother's tone brightened. "That's wonderful. It's been ages since you've done anything fun. You'd have a marvelous time."

Jenny wasn't so sure about that, but she could practically hear her mother's smile, so wasn't going to do anything to dissipate that. They finished talking then she hung up her phone.

Alone. For the whole weekend. Maybe she should volunteer to work.

Or she really could go rafting with her friends and pretend for one weekend that she was a carefree mid-twenties woman who was embracing life.

CHAPTER FOUR

TRISTAN HAD NEVER seen Jenny in anything other than her nursing uniforms. He'd not expected her to be wearing scrubs when she and Laura came out of Jenny's house, but he'd not been prepared for seeing her in casual clothes, either. A brightly colored T-shirt, loose shorts, exposing long, toned legs, a long braid, and a worried expression completed her look. The worried aura, he recognized. It was one she wore around him much too often.

Other than the worried look, he liked Jenny out of her work attire.

He liked her house, too. In a tree-lined neighborhood not too far from the hospital, the houses were older, but overall appeared well kept. Jenny's yard boasted a few massive oak trees and some shade-loving plants bordering her driveway. A couple of brightly colored flower baskets hung from her front porch railing and two navy rocking chairs that perfectly matched the window shutters added to the homey feel. A checkered pillow that said "Home Sweet Home" was angled in one of the chairs. A wooden fence blocked the backyard, providing privacy from whatever she had hidden back there. Was Jenny a hot-tub-on-the-deck person or perhaps an avidly extreme gardener?

Their gazes met and he smiled, hoping she'd do the same. She didn't.

He might be looking forward to this time to get to know her better outside of work, but she didn't feel the same. At some point over the weekend, he'd let her know that she had nothing to worry about. He was great with just being her friend. Usually, that was what he preferred anyway. He didn't get involved with coworkers, but there was something about Jenny to the point where, had she been interested, he'd make an exception to his rule. Regardless, he didn't want anything serious. Between his parents' crazy marriage and subsequent divorce, and there being too much world to experience to get stuck in one place, he'd never wanted that. Just the thought of being tied down too long made his chest tighten around his lungs.

"Is that it?" He gestured to her single bag then glanced toward her for confirmation.

"Laura assures me that this is all I need to bring." She didn't look convinced. "It's all she had on the list she texted me."

"I've got you covered on everything else," Laura reiterated. "If there's something I've missed, someone at camp will have extra, so quit worrying."

"Do I look worried?" Jenny made a face at her friend and Laura stuck out her tongue then laughed. Something about their camaraderie tugged deep inside Tristan. They'd been friends for years. What did that feel like? To have someone in your life that long? He had friends, he reminded himself. Not friendships like theirs, though. Just people he'd connected to during his short time with them and that he'd maintained a loose relationship with over the years. What would it be like to have someone who knew everything about you and loved you all the same?

Shaking the thought, he reached for Jenny's tightly clutched bag.

"She's right. Other than personal items, everything should be good. Plus, according to the GPS map I was looking at last night, our campsite isn't far from a convenience store. We can always pick up anything needed."

"Good to know." Her fingers slowly releasing her bag, she gave it to him and he packed it into the back of his SUV, along with his gear and the supplies he'd brought.

"I've never camped," she admitted. "Hopefully, I won't be a deadweight."

"You won't be." He'd been looking forward to this time with her since hearing that she was going on the trip.

First giving him an odd look, Jenny went to climb into the back of the SUV.

Laura shook her head. "Let me ride in the back. You know when I'm not driving, I sometimes get motion sickness and that, for whatever reason, I do better in the backseat with headphones on than upfront where I can see out the window."

Wincing at the prospect of riding in the front with him, Jenny hesitated at the door while Laura settled in. Was she going to climb into the back, too, and have him chauffeur them around?

"I'll have my audiobook going, so y'all just ignore me," Laura advised as she motioned for Jenny to climb in then slipped on her headset. "I only have a few hours left and have been dying to get back to this story."

"Be my copilot?" Tristan asked, hoping to put Jenny at ease. "You can keep me on task on these backroads so that I don't make Laura's motion sickness worse. If it gets too bad, we can let her drive and I'll get in the back and let you ladies have the front."

"I— Okay." She climbed into the passenger seat and snapped her seat belt. "Just tell me what you need me to do as the copilot and I'll help however I can."

"Relax," he suggested. It's what he wanted her to do more than anything. To relax and enjoy herself and not get so tense around him.

"That's going to help you drive better?"

"Possibly. I don't want you stressed. This trip is supposed to be fun, so you shouldn't look as if you're headed to the dentist to have your wisdom teeth cut out."

To her credit, she smiled.

"That's better," he encouraged. "Now, if I can just keep you smiling. Want me to tell you corny nursing jokes?"

"Just get us there safe and I promise I'll smile the moment we arrive."

Because then she'd escape being in a vehicle with him? From his peripheral vision he saw her fold her hands in her lap and turn to look out the window. He suspected she wished she had headphones and an audiobook, as well, so she had an excuse to shut him out.

"Find us a radio station?" he suggested, thinking music might be a good icebreaker. Music was always good.

"Sure. What type do you like?"

"Anything is fine, but my favorite is classic rock," he admitted, pulling out of the parking spot.

"As in Led Zeppelin, Aerosmith, the Rolling Stones, the Doors, and that type of classic rock?" She sounded surprised.

Glancing her way, Tristan grinned. Who knew she'd be a classic rock fan, too? "Who's your favorite?"

"I grew up listening to a lot of Eagles and Fleetwood Mac with my mom and now I find myself smiling a little on the inside any time I hear something by either group."

His love of music had developed opposite from hers, more of an escape from reality than something to ground him to it. Music had been a constant in his life, his familiar friend when starting over somewhere new.

"Does your mother live close?" he asked for a distraction from his thoughts as much as curiosity about Jenny's life.

"Very." Amusement laced her tone. "We live in the same house."

Interesting and not something that he could imagine willingly doing at her age. Or at any age that he was old enough to have done otherwise.

"That is close."

"Honestly, I don't know what I'd do without her." Genuine love and appreciation oozed from her words. "She's a nurse at a local assisted-living home."

"Does living together make dating difficult?"

"Not at all. She dates regularly."

Tristan chuckled. "I was referring to you."

"I've already told you that I don't date."

"But your mother does?"

"Yes. She has a boyfriend. I suspect they'll marry at some point, and I'm great with that. She deserves every good thing, and he makes her happy. He works with her at the assisted-living facility, but he's in the office." She tapped her fingers against her thighs in rhythm with the radio's beat. "How did we get on this topic?"

"What do you want to talk about?"

"With you?" Her question revealed too much for his liking, but finally she shrugged. "Tell me about being a travel nurse. Where's the coolest place you've worked?"

"Maine," he answered without hesitation. "I'd put in for a rotation in Alaska, but that didn't pan out. At the time, I didn't have as much experience as the hospital there wanted. If something opens up, I may try again. I'd like to spend time around Juneau."

She twisted a little in her seat to more fully look at him. "Apparently, we have poor communication skills as I'd actually used the term 'cool' to mean awesome rather than temperature. But tell me about Maine."

"Cool is too mild a description for my time in Maine. I worked inland, fairly close to the Canadian border, in a small-town hospital. My rotation was from fall until late spring. It was cold, sometimes we'd get twelve inches of snow at a time, and it never warmed up enough for it to melt away, so it just kept building upon itself until spring."

"I don't think I'd like that."

"It was great by me since I knew I wasn't staying long term. I went to experience the snow, skiing, and to just take in the frozen beauty of the area. It's a gorgeous place."

"If you say so. I'm not a fan of being cold." She rubbed her arms to emphasize her point. "Is there somewhere you intend to eventually take a permanent hospital position?"

Just the thought of being trapped in one location made his throat tighten.

"No. I don't see myself staying anywhere more than a year maximum. I like the three- to six-month rotations I'm on. It's a great timeframe for checking out the area and finding hidden treasures away from the usual tourist spots."

In a couple of months, his Chattanooga contract would be up, and he'd be moving on to his next location. Chicago had made a nice offer, as had Wisconsin, but he'd not yet decided. Maybe for three months at one or the other, though, and then he could take a spot somewhere Deep South for the winter months rather than heading further north.

"I can't imagine moving around so much."

Tristan couldn't imagine not. What would it be

like to come home to the same place night after night, week after week, month after month, year after year? He liked his studio apartment, but it was just a place to sleep. Clearing his throat, he said, "I like seeing the world."

"That's what the internet and television are for," she countered.

Something in the way she said it had him asking, "You're kidding, right?"

She didn't say anything.

"You don't like traveling? Seeing the world first-person rather than through someone else's perspective?"

"I'm happy in Chattanooga," Jenny attested. "I have a good life here."

Then the truth, as much as it boggled his mind, hit him. "Have you ever been out of Chattanooga, Jenny?"

"Of course, I've been out of Chattanooga. To Atlanta a few times and Nashville."

Claustrophobia clawed at him at how confined she'd been. "Is that it? What about vacations?"

"Those were vacations," she said, her tone defensive.

"We need to get you out of Chattanooga and let you see the world," Tristan mused.

Jenny shook her head. "My world is in Chattanooga."

"Yeah, but—"

"Seriously, this isn't an argument you can win. You do you and have no roots. I like my roots and that they run deep. Chattanooga is my home. My family is here. I'm happy here."

Awe that she had meant what she'd said, that she really was happy within her small geographical bubble, shook him. Jenny truly didn't care if she traveled beyond her immediate circle. Her roots bound her as surely as if they encased her within their treacherous tentacles.

Or maybe they grounded her so the strongest wind couldn't topple her resolve.

"I didn't mean to offend you," he said and meant it.

"You didn't. You… Okay, so maybe I was defensive. Sorry."

"It's good that you feel so passionate about your home."

"This coming from the guy who just said he wasn't ever settling down anywhere."

"That doesn't mean I can't appreciate that you're passionate about where you live. Besides, I've always heard that home is where the heart is."

"And your heart is only home for three to six months at a time?"

Had his heart ever been in any of the places he'd lived?

"Don't knock it until you try it," he advised, not liking how their conversation kept making him question himself, when it was she who should be questioning her life choices. Who stayed within a hundred miles of where they were born their entire lives? "There's something liberating about seeing the world."

"There's something comforting about the familiar, too," she countered. "A few years back, our landlord decided to sell the house my mom had rented most of my life. The one where you picked me up this morning. With the help of the bank, I bought it. I love the way walking through its doors makes me feel."

Why did listening to her make him feel as if he'd been the one deprived, rather than her?

Taking a deep breath, he swallowed the knot in his throat. "How's that?"

"Proud. At peace. Safe." Her voice became almost nostalgic. "Loved."

Jenny didn't see her house as just a place to sleep, but more of an extension of who she was.

Roots. Hers were deeply embedded and gave her strength. Unease settled in his stomach. Unease that what she'd described was as foreign to him as living out of a suitcase was to her.

"Are you a Braves fan?"

Twisting in her seat to look at him again, she hesitated, making him wonder if she'd picked up on how uncomfortable their conversation had made him.

Rather than pry, she nodded. "Is there any other team?"

Breathing a little easier, he laughed. "Maybe we could catch a game."

Was he asking her on a date or suggesting going with their work crew on another group trip? As foolish as he considered the conversation they'd just had, and knowing she was more apt to agree to a group activity, if pressed, he'd have to admit he wanted it to be just the two of them.

"Have you been to a Braves' game before?" she asked rather than comment on his invitation.

"I've seen them play but not in the Atlanta stadium. I caught them in Boston."

He and a neighborhood kid had snuck in to watch the game. Rollo hadn't been the best influence, so it was just as well they hadn't stayed in that apartment long. Thinking back, he tried to summon the warm fuzzies Jenny got over her home and couldn't. Instead, he barely recalled which apartment they'd even lived in at the time.

"Did you do a rotation in Boston, then?"

He shook his head. "I lived there during my early teen years."

"Is that where you're from? Massachusetts?"

"I'm not from anywhere. We moved a lot." They'd moved so often, he'd sometimes felt as if his real home was the backseat of his father's beat-up king cab truck or whatever junker his mother had sweet-talked off a boyfriend.

"Your parents liked to travel, too?" Jenny asked, pulling him from the past.

"You could say that." His parents hadn't traveled to see the world, though. His mother's moves had had more to do with escaping creditors and ex-boyfriends. A tradition she'd continued until the day she'd died during his last year in nursing school. His father had worked construction, still did; wherever the next job took him was where Travis Scott resided.

"My dad left before I was born," Jenny surprised him by saying. She safeguarded everything personal so much that the insight to who she was felt like a precious gift. "Mom didn't have money for travel, but I never did without anything and was rich in love. She's my rock."

Rich in love? There went that weird feeling in his stomach again.

Tristan stared ahead at the winding road that snaked along the river. He tapped his fingers on the steering wheel to the music's beat. The melody failed to calm him. Not once had he thought of his mother or father as his rock, nor had he ever felt rich in love. Most of his childhood, he'd felt more like a millstone around their necks, dragging them down with his presence.

Maybe if he'd had Jenny's idyllic-sounding childhood, he'd feel at home somewhere and want to stay. But nowhere had ever felt like home. He doubted it ever would, which was just as well since he preferred being footloose and fancy-free. The world was a big place and he wanted to see it all.

"I can't just stand here doing nothing," Jenny insisted after they'd checked in at their campsite. They, along with Roger and his girlfriend, who'd fallen in behind their car on the drive, were the first from their group to arrive, but the others were close. "I need to help."

"Roger, Lucia and I have our tent," Laura assured her, spreading out the nylon material. Then, with a grin, suggested, "See if Tristan needs help."

Of course, her friend wanted her to help Tristan.

She glanced toward where he was setting up his tent. Roger and Lucia's tent was to the left of Jenny and Laura's. Tristan's was quite a ways back from the others. Jenny bit into her lower lip.

She didn't want to be thrown together with him all weekend, but apparently that was what was going to happen. She should have gone to the aquarium with her mother and Sawyer.

Or maybe she just needed to relax and quit worrying so much. It didn't matter how much she was thrown together with Tristan. Nothing was going to happen. Nothing like what her friend was hoping, at any rate.

Chatting with Tristan on the ride had been… well, not horrible. He was interesting and, once they'd gotten beyond the topic of travel and his one awkward period where he'd changed the subject and she'd kept wondering what he was thinking of, he'd made her laugh. Mostly with corny nurse jokes. But laughing with him had felt…good.

Taking a deep breath, she walked the thirty yards or so to where his tent was set up on the opposite side of the fire pit, near the outskirts of the campsite. Had he purposely chosen to be further away? Or maybe he thought that when the others arrived they'd fill the gaps?

"Laura sent me to help," she said, not wanting him to read her being there wrong. Friendly, but not too friendly. That's what she was going for.

"Thanks." He half smiled, digging a dimple into his cheek. "You want to gather some kindling? I brought a few bigger pieces, but we'll need smaller sticks to get our fire started for later tonight."

It wasn't chilly but the temp would drop once the sun set. A fire would feel good. Plus, what was camping without a campfire? She should learn all she could so that she could take Sawyer without being totally lost. She had to start looking at this trip the right way. It was research. "If you'll show me an example of what we need, I'll help."

He found a handful of small sticks and pine needles. "Anything like this would be great.

We'll get enough for tonight and tomorrow night."

Jenny gathered sticks, stacking a small pile next to the block-edged area where they'd build their fire. Several others had arrived and were unloading their wares, setting up their tents and laughing. She greeted her coworkers, met their significant others for the ones who'd brought a plus-one, then went off to gather more fire-starting wood, searching through the nearby trees for various-sized pieces.

"Finding much?" Tristan asked.

Jenny held up her sticks. "I've got a pretty good pile going next to the fire pit. I wasn't sure how much we'd need, so thought I'd get a bit more, just in case."

"Sounds like a good plan. Allergic to poison ivy?" he asked, motioning to her wares.

"Not that I know of." Her palms instantly starting to itch, she glanced down at the wood. She had a general idea of what the plant looked like, was well aware of what the rash looked like from her nursing school days of working in the emergency room, but she was far from an expert on poisonous vegetation. "Is that what I'm holding?"

"No, but it is what's growing on that tree next to you. I wasn't sure if you'd noticed and didn't want you rubbing against it in hope of a reason to get out of the trip tomorrow."

"Oh. Right. Sorry." She backed away from the tree. "I've never had a reaction, but I've never gone tromping through the woods, either. Although getting out of the rafting trip tomorrow sounds tempting, I'm not a fan of itchy rashes."

"I hear you." Picking up a medium-sized branch that had fallen from a tree, he placed his foot on the limb for stabilization and snapped it into more manageable pieces. "It's hard to imagine living here and not spending a lot of time outdoors."

"I didn't say that I didn't spend a lot of time outdoors, just that I haven't gone tromping through the woods," she clarified, bending to pick up another stick.

From spring to fall, she mowed their lawn weekly then tended to their flower beds. Seeing the brightly colored blooms adding splashes of color made her happy. Her mother, too. Other than the garden box that she'd let Sawyer plant vegetable seeds in and their small above-ground bed she'd bought at a local home supply store,

Sawyer didn't seem to care one way or the other about their landscaping efforts. However, he did love their trips to a nearby playground on her days off and when the weather permitted.

"Watch for snakes," Tristan warned.

Jenny froze. "Snakes? No one mentioned snakes."

Sleeping in a tent took on a new, unpleasant twist. If she slept at all.

"They won't bother you unless you bother them," Tristan continued, "but keep an eye out on where you're stepping and picking up sticks. I don't want you accidentally startling one and getting bit."

She didn't move. "I'm nervous enough already and now you mention snakes. Someone should have warned me. All this time, I thought the river was the biggest danger."

"Don't be nervous, Jenny. I just wanted you to be careful but didn't mean to make you worried." He touched her shoulder and shockwaves shot through her. Just a simple touch, with her cotton T-shirt separating their skin, and yet every nerve ending within her focused on what he'd meant to be a comforting gesture. Her head spinning, she stepped back to steady herself.

"We probably won't see any," he noted, "but I promise I'll fend off any snake we encounter."

Although he was teasing, she had no doubt that he would. That truth shone in his eyes and did funny things to her belly. She'd never had a man in her life who'd promised to protect her. From a crawling reptile or anything else. That she believed Tristan would, at least for the weekend, had her clearing her throat and taking another step back. She didn't need some wannabe white knight messing with her world.

"You're the only thing I'm worried about fending off," she admitted, trying to stop the softening in her chest. She absolutely could not fall for him. To do so was nothing short of emotional suicide. He was leaving in less than three months. Here today, gone tomorrow.

Face pinching, he shook his head. "There you go with that stellar impression of me again. Someday you're going to realize I'm not that bad."

Guilt hit. She hadn't meant to offend him. Or maybe she had, to put some emotional distance between them. During the drive, once they'd quit talking about personal things and had just been chatting, relaxing had been much too easy. She needed to keep up her guard. Not only that, to stay on the offensive to actively fight to protect her heart.

With that in mind, she straightened her shoulders. “Don’t count on it.”

Curiosity shone in his eyes. “Because?”

Because the way you make me feel terrifies me. Because the way my heart pounds when you’re near leaves me near breathless. Because the way my insides dance when our eyes meet throws me off kilter. Because the way I can’t stop thinking about you rattles my logic.

“Because I suspect you’re not that good, either.”

Too bad she didn’t believe her own claim. There were things she suspected he would be very good at. Her eyes dropped to his mouth, flashbacks of her dream—*dreams!*—hitting her.

He’s a terrible kisser, she told herself. *Horrible. The worst.*

“You might be right on the ‘not being that good,’” he chuckled, “but I like to think I’m a decent guy.”

Visions of him kissing her, asking her how that one was, had her swallowing hard. None of it was real.

Knowing he had no clue where her crazy thoughts had just gone, she shook her head. "You'll be gone long before you'll have time to convince me of that."

Thank goodness, because maybe then she'd quit thinking about him, quit wondering about his lips and how bad or good they were.

But when her gaze met his and her stomach fluttered with the intensity of a riled hornet's nest, she wondered if it was already too late for him to not fill her mind and dreams.

CHAPTER FIVE

LAURA HAD BROUGHT an extra fold-up chair and blanket for Jenny, and along with most of the group, they sat around the campfire, basking in its glow and listening to Tristan.

Jenny hadn't known he played the guitar. She also hadn't known he sang. Then again, why would she?

Perhaps it was the influence of how her hormones reacted to him, but his smooth tone lent itself well to the Eagles' "One of These Nights."

Several chimed in during the chorus, but Jenny remained silent. Had he purposely chosen the number due to their conversation during their drive? Or due to the lyrics?

The warm flicker of the fire was plenty to ward off the mild night's chill, but Jenny liked the feel of the fuzzy blanket. Perhaps because having it wrapped loosely around her body made her feel shielded from what was happening to her every time Tristan glanced her way.

"You ready to admit he's hot?" Laura whispered.

Jenny snorted, glancing to where her bestie sat next to her. "I thought I already had. Besides, was his hotness ever really in question?"

Laura laughed. "Y'all seemed to be getting along during the drive."

"We were discussing the weather."

"Yeah, right. I wasn't so into my audiobook that I didn't notice you laughing. Since when has Tennessee weather been humorous?"

He had made her laugh. "Can I help it if he kept telling dumb jokes? Eventually, he wore me down and I started laughing in hopes he'd stop."

"Right." Laura's look shifted to Tristan. "So, you admit he's hot and he makes you laugh." She flashed her eyebrows. "I think you should go for it this weekend."

Wrapping the blanket tighter around her, Jenny gulped before hesitantly asking, "Go for what?"

"Him," Laura said without hesitation. "He seems a great guy. And before you start in with your arguments, so what if he's not going to be here long? You're a single mom who never does anything for herself. This weekend is all about you, not Sawyer or work or anything except *you*. Why not have some fun for a change?"

"You say that as if I'm miserable. I'm not. And, even if I was, I certainly don't need a man to have fun. That's what the entire weekend is supposed to be about. Me having fun." Jenny bared her teeth in a cheesy smile. "This is me having fun."

"The life of the party," Laura teased. "I've watched you keep your nose to the grind for years now, Jen. I know you love being a mom, that Sawyer makes you happy, and that you like your job. But the reality is that spending your time with Tristan is another type of fun."

"Yeah, the kind of fun that led to me being a single mom while still in college," she reminded her. "No thank you. I wouldn't trade Sawyer for anything in the world, but I don't need more of that particular fun in my life."

Laura shrugged. "There are ways of preventing pregnancy."

"Which sometimes don't work. You know it's not the single-mom part that's the problem. It's the headache of a man in my life and all the drama that involves." And the heartache because she had been crushed at the depth of Geoffrey's deception. Engaged to another woman, one he'd gone on to marry just as planned. How could Jenny have been so blind? How had his fiancée so easily accepted his infidelity and married him anyway? And then Carlos, who'd realized he didn't want to be involved with a single mom. Or maybe he'd known all along and had just used her while he'd had the chance. Either way, he'd left. "No thanks."

"What drama? It's been eons since you've dated."

"I don't have to have been on a date to have witnessed the drama. You go through it every time you have a new boyfriend." At Laura's look of disbelief, Jenny elaborated. "There's the elation phase, where you're walking in the clouds because you're so infatuated. Then there's the reality part, where you settle into the relationship. Then there's the breakup, where the world becomes gloom and doom. After that, you repeat the cycle." She shook her head. "That's not for me. Not again. Not when I know how much it hurts. Not when I have Sawyer to think about."

Wincing, Laura stared. "Girl, when did you become so cynical?"

They both knew.

"You call it cynical." Jenny shrugged. "I call it being realistic."

"There are people who find true love," Laura insisted.

"Yeah, well, none of the people I know have, at least, not the romantic kind." But she did know true love. She never doubted that her mother and her son loved her with all their hearts. She gave her friend a pointed look. "I'm including you and me in that lack of romantic true love."

"It's not from lack of trying on my part," Laura refuted. "Someday I will find a man who appreciates all this." She waved her hand up and down her curvy body. "But I disagree with you that we don't know someone truly in love. Look at Roger and Lucia. They're happy."

Jenny glanced at the couple roasting marshmallows over the fire. Every so often, they'd share a special look and, yeah, that was love in their regard for one another. Or, more likely, lust. "They're still in the honeymoon phase. Give them time."

"They've been together for years and are perfect together," Laura pointed out. "How did I not realize how deeply this cynicism went?"

"After Carlos, I decided it was best to avoid

the dating cesspool. No need to dive in with the first pretty face that comes along." A pretty face attached to a fit body that held a good work ethic, a kind heart and a humorous personality, but who was keeping tabs?

"Say what you will, but Tristan Scott's a cesspool I don't mind bathing in."

At her friend's suggestive eyebrow waggle, Jenny snorted. "I personally prefer the shower houses we passed on our way in."

Laura nudged her. "Take my advice, and you won't need a cold shower."

The following morning, despite her awareness of the man sitting to her left on the wooden bench, Jenny focused on everything the instructor was reviewing on white-water rafting safety.

"You okay?"

She cut her eyes to Tristan but didn't answer. She didn't want to risk missing some key information that might save her if she came out of the raft.

Lord, please don't let me fall out of the raft.

Keep her hand over the end of her paddle at all times so that she didn't allow it to hit another rafter or lose it. Never put her feet down if she fell out of the raft because she could get trapped in the rocks and the current would then push her under. Keep her life jacket on at all times—no worries on that one. Listen to what her guide said at all times. Yep, that one wouldn't be a problem, either. She'd be hanging on to the instructor's every word.

Only, apparently, their raft wouldn't have a guide from the outdoor center.

"What do you mean we qualify to go down without a guide?" she asked a few minutes later when Roger made the announcement. She didn't share his excitement.

"Tristan was an instructor in Colorado," Laura told her. "Same difference."

"No, it's not. We aren't in Colorado," Jenny countered, anxiety rising. "We need someone familiar with this river. Not one halfway across the country."

"Relax, Jenny. Lucia and I are experienced rafters," Roger promised. "Of our group, you're the only one who has never been down the river. Most have been several times. The river's water level is average today. We've got this."

Jenny bit into her lower lip, her eyes going back and forth between her friends and settling on where Tristan tightened his life jacket strap. He'd remained quiet during her protests. When his gaze lifted to hers, she wondered if she'd see annoyance at her protests, or perhaps humor at her worries. Instead, concern shone in his blue depths. Not concern over the trip, but that same protective gleam that had shone when he'd promised to keep her safe from any snakes they might encounter.

"It'll be okay, Jenny," Lucia assured her, giving her a quick hug and drawing her attention from Tristan. "I was just as nervous when Roger brought me for the first time a few years back. We've made several trips now and always have a great time."

Heart still pounding at the look she'd shared with Tristan, she focused on Roger's girlfriend. "But you had a guide all those times, right?"

"We have a guide this time, too," Laura, Lucia and Roger said at the same time and then laughed.

The others just smiled and went about making sure their life jackets were on and appropriately snug. They were her friends. She trusted that they wouldn't put her in undue danger. And yet…

“Here, let me check your life jacket,” Tristan offered, coming over to her.

“Please do. I’ve never had a reason to wear one and may have gotten it wrong,” Jenny said.

“Life jackets are pretty basic. You’re a quick learner and did a great job,” he confirmed even as he gave her strap a tight tug. “Relax and have fun, Jenny. I’m not going to let anything happen to you.”

There he went making promises to protect her again.

Sucking as deep a breath as the snug life jacket would allow, she nodded. As crazy as it was, she believed that he’d truly do his best to keep anything from happening to her.

Unfortunately, there were some things beyond his control.

“I know you’ll do your best to keep me safe,” she admitted, staring up at him, wishing he’d step back considering how close he was from where he’d adjusted her strap. When he didn’t, she stepped back, but stumbled.

On cue, Tristan’s hand grasped her arm, steadying her. “You okay?”

No, her mind screamed. Even through the rubbery raincoat the outfitter had supplied to go under her life jacket, the heat of his touch burned her, threatened to have her stumbling around with the shockwaves of it.

"Fine." She pulled her arm free. "Thank you."

"Anytime." His smile was electric, lighting up his eyes with amusement. "For the record, you look cute in your helmet."

Tugging on her chin strap, she rolled her eyes. "Has no one ever told you that women don't want to be called cute?"

"Not that I recall," he admitted, looking amused. "Would you be okay with me telling you that you're beautiful?"

Heat singed her cheeks. She doubted that even the most iconic beauties could look great while wearing her current gear, but she forced a smile. "Thank you. For the compliment, for checking my vest, and for keeping me upright. Make sure to tell me if I'm not doing something right today. I don't want to put us in danger with my inexperience."

Reaching out, he cupped her face, his thumb brushing over her chin strap and sending shivers all up and down her spine. "You're going to do fine, Jenny, and by the end of the day you're going to be a pro."

* * *

Finally, Jenny seemed to be relaxing. Tristan had caught her laughing a couple of times at something Laura said, but mostly she kept glaring and rolling her eyes at her friend. Their raft had the five of them. Roger and Lucia were at the front. Jenny and Laura took the middle, so they wouldn't get hammered by the waves quite as much, and he was at the back. Roger and Lucia had done a great job following his called-out instructions, so they'd hit the rapids at just the right spots to avoid the many rocks that jutted up or were semi hidden beneath the surface.

"Keep your hand around the T-grip." Tristan spoke loud enough over the rapids for Jenny to hear as their raft made a few up and downs over a fast, bumpy section. He didn't want the end of her oar smacking him or anyone else in the face.

"Got it," Jenny responded, wrapping her hand back around the tip she'd momentarily let go of. She'd been holding on to it so tightly earlier that he was surprised she'd let go.

"Everyone, paddle hard right," he called, guiding them through a rocky section.

"Woohoo!" Roger cheered, holding up his oar

when they exited the rapid to a calm section. "That was awesome."

From his position behind them, Tristan saw Jenny nod, heard her laughter, and relief filled him. He wanted her to enjoy today. Whether or not she did mattered more than it should. He loved the sport and wanted… What did it matter what she thought? He was only here a short time.

"From what I learned when studying the river last night, we have a short stretch of calm before we hit the next rapids. Anyone ready to pull over to shore for a snack and rest break?"

"Sounds great," a few called out.

He directed them to a flat pebbly shoreline. When close enough, Roger jumped out into the midcalf-deep water and guided the raft up onto the rocks enough that the others could disembark without stepping directly into the water. Once they were out, Tristan got out, too, pulling the raft even further up on the pebble bed so they didn't have to worry about the boat taking off without them.

"Here's sanitizer," Laura said, passing around a small spray bottle.

Smiling, looking a little cold from the icy water, Jenny had sat on a downed tree trunk along the edge of the bank and had her face lifted toward the sun.

"Having a good time?"

Keeping her face raised and eyed closed, she said, "Much better than I was expecting when we pushed off this morning."

"That's not saying a lot," he quipped, knowing the answer to his question by how the earlier stiffness of her movements was gone and she looked at peace with the sunlight brightening her face. Angelic, he thought. And so beautiful with the tiny curling-from-dampness hairs that had escaped her ponytail framing her face and her full lips slightly parted.

Longing to touch them sucker-punched him, threatened to drag him over to her, so he could taste their lushness for himself. Wincing, he mentally plunged himself into the icy river.

"True. My expectations were pretty low," she admitted. "I didn't think I'd like going over the rapids, but it's exhilarating."

The excitement shining in her eyes was exhilarating and had him wondering if he was going to have to take a real dunk into the water.

"I enjoy the rapids the most, but only because there's balance," he confessed. "It's like life.

There are times of peace and calm, and times of fighting to keep from being swept away. It takes both to fully appreciate each moment."

"You're giving me a philosophy lesson based upon white-water rafting?" She looked at him with laughter in her eyes.

The amusement in her honey-brown eyes triggered an excitement within him that far surpassed any the rapids had produced. "Maybe, but it's true. One only appreciates the calm points because of the times of adversity." Knowing he needed to break eye contact before he started spouting poetry to go along with his philosophy, he turned from her and opened a waterproof bag where he'd packed snacks and drinks. Laura hadn't seemed to mind when he'd asked for details on what Jenny liked and he'd told her that he had Jenny's rafting trip covered.

"We have lunch packed for a later stop, but we'll all be grateful for our meal tonight. We're grilling burgers." He handed her a water bottle that he'd had clipped to the raft. "This is yours. I should have told you that earlier."

Seeming surprised that he'd brought her one, she smiled. "Thank you."

"You're welcome."

Taking the bottle, she twisted the top off. Tristan's eyes were mesmerized by the working of her throat as she took a long sip then glanced his way. "How did you end up as a rafting guide?"

"It was during the summer of my freshman and sophomore year of college."

"Is that where you attended college? In Colorado?"

He shook his head. "I started university in Virginia but ended up finishing my nursing program in California."

"California? After spending at least part of your teens in Boston? Good grief, you really have lived all over. So, while you were living in Virginia for college, you spent your summers working in Colorado? How did that happen?"

"My dorm mate was from there and was working as a guide on the Colorado River. It didn't take much for him to convince me I should get trained and work with him." Staying in the same place for his nursing school had been the longest time he'd lived in one location. Spending the summers elsewhere had helped his itchy feet. "It was a great experience."

"The Colorado River sounds intense."

"After some of the rapids we crossed today, I'm surprised that you're saying that, but the truth is that even a calm-appearing river can be dangerous if not respected. You never know what's lurking beneath the surface."

"Did anyone ever get hurt on your watch?"

"Just once when a guy let go of his T-grip and busted up his friend's mouth."

Jenny winced. "Poor guy."

"That's one of the most important things to remember when in the boat."

"And keeping my toes up is one of the most important things to remember if I fall out of the boat?"

"It is *the* most important thing to remember if you're out of the boat," he corrected, not liking the thought of Jenny falling out. "Let's keep you in the raft and not have to worry about where your toes are."

"I'm great with that plan."

"Me, too."

He handed her a trail mix packet then grabbed one for himself. "Here. You need sustenance. You've got a lot of paddling to do before the day is done."

Jenny turned up the bag, pouring a generous

helping of the mix into her mouth. "Mmm..." She licked salt from her lips. "That's good."

"That's hunger talking." Hunger was talking to him, too. Loud and demanding and with an urgency that had him thinking he should go dunk his head in the chilly river to abate his thoughts, pronto.

"Maybe," she agreed then glanced at where he sat next to her. "Thank you for taking care of me today. I haven't exactly been a bundle of friendliness, so I particularly appreciate you making sure I stay safe, and for my water and snack."

Pleasure filled him. Not that he wanted her ingratiated to him, but he liked that she was looking at him with a smile in her eyes and on her mouth.

His glance dropped to her lips. Her full lips that she must have thought had another bit of salt on them because she licked them again.

Fighting the urge to groan, Tristan took a sip of his water. The cool liquid went down wrong and triggered a coughing spell as he tried to swallow.

"You okay over there?" Roger called from where he, Lucia and Laura were having their snack.

"Fine," he assured him between coughs. "Water went down the wrong way."

"Don't get choked up or Jenny will have to resuscitate you," Roger teased.

Jenny giving him mouth-to-mouth would be worth getting choked up.

When he turned back, she was studying the water as if it was extremely interesting, but overall, she seemed relaxed. He'd count that as an improvement.

Had he not already known, the way his new coworkers purposely kept pushing him and Jenny together, leaving them semi alone, would have clued him in to their approval of something happening between them.

Too bad Jenny didn't agree, because the more Tristan got to know her, the more he wanted something to happen, too.

Jenny followed Tristan's instructions, keeping her hand tightly over the T-grip as he told the group to paddle hard right or left.

Adrenaline filled her as they surged through the river, as they battled one rapid after another and came out the other side. Yeah, she could see how people enjoyed taking on the elements and feeling as if they'd conquered something with every bend of the river successfully navigated.

Not that she'd want to go back, but she'd be lying if she said she was as miserable as she'd thought she'd be when she'd let her friends convince her to go.

You wanted to go. Admit it, a voice inside her prompted. *You wanted to see the man behind you away from the hospital. To see what he was like away from the constraints of work.*

That meant what? she wondered while paddling in whatever direction he instructed.

He was an excellent guide, always calm, always precise and loud enough with his orders to be heard without being overbearing or outright yelling except when the sound of the water was deafening around them. He was like that at work, too. Was that how he was in all aspects of life? Calm, focused, able to guide those around them to keep them safe?

"Roger, do you see what I see?" Tristan called out, referring to a group ahead. Their raft, along with a couple of rafters in the water, floated far down the river without the remainder.

Her feet lodged as far beneath the seat in front of her as she could get them tucked, Jenny's stomach sank as they got closer and closer to a man propped against a boulder, stretched out toward a person who wasn't moving. Just beyond, two rafters had somehow made it to shore and were motioning to the ones in the water with the rapids bubbling fast around them.

"Hard right," Tristan ordered, pointing their raft in the direction of the shore and the people. The water rushed, but it wasn't the fastest or bumpiest area they'd traversed, and they managed to maneuver near to where the rafters were in the water and shot straight on top of a boulder, causing their raft to get stuck about fifteen feet from where the closest rafter stood.

"Oh, God," she prayed, helplessness washing over her as she realized the closest rafter was a teen girl and she appeared stuck. Her fingers gripped some type of greenery growing in the water and Jenny suspected that desperate hold was the only thing keeping her from being pushed beneath the water.

Grabbing a bag Jenny hadn't previously paid any attention to, Tristan moved to the front of their stuck raft, swapping places with Roger's girlfriend, who quickly moved to the back of the raft.

"Everyone okay?" he called. They didn't look okay to Jenny, but she supposed asking was protocol just as asking was the first thing one did with CPR.

"A man went overboard and, in my efforts to get him, our raft got stuck and capsized. Kira's foot is trapped. I'm not stuck, but not able to get to her. Every time I move forward, the water slams me back into this boulder," the man in the water answered. He was positioned to use one of the large rocks for leverage to stay put. One arm held on to the rock and the other was stretched to the girl, but she was beyond his reach. "I almost got swept down the river the last time I tried."

Turning his attention to the teen, Tristan asked, "Kira, are you hurt?"

The quivering girl didn't answer, just stared at them with panic in her eyes. Panic and yet distance shone in her gaze, too. Hypothermia or shock or both?

"Kira, we're going to get you loose," Tristan promised. "You're too far away to reach my oar for me to pull you into our raft, so I'm going to toss a rope to you. I'll throw it upriver. The water will bring it to you. I need you to grab hold."

Seeming to come out of her haze, the girl nodded. "I'm so cold."

The splashes of water were frigid, and Jenny could only imagine how cold the teen was, being submerged up to just beneath her breasts.

He tossed the rope, but the girl watched the end go by without letting go of the greenery she clung to. Tristan pulled the rope back up.

"Kira, I know it's scary to let go, but I need you to grab hold of the rope so I can get you in our raft. Are you ready?"

The girl hesitated but finally nodded. Tristan tossed the rope, and with a held breath, Jenny watched the end float past the petrified girl again.

"I—I can't do it."

"You can," Tristan reassured her, his voice so confident that he almost convinced Jenny of the girl's ability.

"I'm so cold that my arms won't work," Kira said.

Tristan looked to Roger. They seemed to share some secret guy code and the next thing Jenny knew, Tristan had gone into the water, him holding one end of the rope and Roger having the other, securing it.

"No!" Jenny couldn't contain her cry as Tristan battled the water to close the short distance to the girl.

Fear seized her. This. This was what she'd been afraid of, and they'd all made light of her concerns. She'd let loose, let herself enjoy the ride, and now Tristan was in the water and the young girl was ghostly white and looking as if she were about to lose consciousness.

"Be careful," she whispered, her breath catching as Tristan made it to the series of rocks jutting up from the water. He used a rock to propel himself toward the teenager.

"Yes!" Laura cheered when he got stopped a few feet from where the girl was taking a beating from the water around her.

Jenny's throat was too constricted to say anything. Watching him bob around in the bubbly water had her nerves a wreck.

Rope secure, Tristan made his way to the teen. When he reached her, everyone let loose with whoops and hollers. Everyone but Jenny because reaching the trapped girl wasn't enough. They were both still in the water, along with the other raft's guide. The water hadn't magically stopped to let them leisurely get the girl loose. They were still in danger.

She'd cheer when they were safely out of the water.

CHAPTER SIX

"YOUR NAME IS KIRA?" Tristan asked the trapped teen as he assessed the situation to see how to free her while keeping himself safe in the process. The water shot around him, threatening to pull him along with its powerful force.

"Yes," she said, her teeth chattering. Panic and fatigue shone in her eyes from her battling to stay upright.

The current was strong, whipping at Tristan, and creating a struggle to close the small gap between him and the girl. One slipup and he could end up with his own foot trapped. He wouldn't let the consequences of that happening into his mind. He needed to focus.

"Hi, Kira. My name is Tristan. I'm going to get you out of the water." Somehow, he would. "Talk to me about what's going on beneath the surface. Are both feet trapped or just one?"

"Just my right one."

Good. Maybe she'd be able to help push herself free when they made their move. "Tell me what you feel."

"I can't feel anything except cold."

She probably hadn't been in the water long prior to their coming upon the group since they'd been able to see the raft and the two who had floated down the river. But the water was cold and, if it hadn't already, it wouldn't take long for hypothermia to set in.

"I'm going to free your foot, Kira, but you're going to have to help me so that I don't injure you further when I'm pulling you free. Can you do that?"

She nodded.

Water swirled around them. The current tugged at him as he tried to maintain a secure footing of his own in an attempt to get an idea of where Kira was trapped and how best to free her. He had no visual of how she was wedged. If he pulled wrong, he could break her ankle, if it wasn't already, or he could cause the rocks to cut her, or any number of other injuries. When it came down to it, he might not have a choice, but if there was a way that he could free her without further injury, he'd do his best. Maybe he'd get lucky, and he'd be able to move the rock trapping her enough so that she could wiggle her foot free.

The water roared deafeningly around him, blocking out all other sound as he maneuvered on the rocks. Almost, he was close enough. Just another step—

Surprising him, Kira lost her grip on the greenery. Knowing he only had a tiny window for success before she'd be forced beneath the water, he grabbed at her life jacket, barely catching hold of the strap and lifting her up.

Sobbing, Kira stared at him with wide, scared eyes.

Fighting to keep his footing, he lashed the end of the rope through her life jacket. "Once I have your foot loose, my friend Roger will pull you to our raft."

Tristan got the rope secured around her, to where, if it took him a while to free her, at least Roger could keep enough tension in the rope to keep her upright. The water around them was too deep for him to free her foot with his hands without his going under water, which would mean him battling the current and his life jacket. Even if he could, the water was too murky and aeriated for visibility. He had to use his energy wisely.

Using his foot as a guide, he realized she was trapped beneath a jagged edge of the large boulder. He wouldn't be moving the rock, but maybe he could help her wiggle her foot free without causing further damage than whatever she'd already sustained.

"At my signal, and with as much strength as you can, I want you to force your foot in the direction you think it needs to go to be free."

Shivering, Kira nodded, and Tristan called to Roger, "At my signal, pull the rope with all your might."

At Roger's thumbs-up, Tristan took one last deep breath then went for it, knowing that if he didn't free Kira, it might be impossible for him to regain a decent footing for a second attempt, leaving them no choice but to forcibly dislodge her regardless of the cost to her foot.

"Now!" he yelled as with all his strength he pushed them in the opposite direction from the water flow and upward into the tug of the rope, praying it worked.

By some miracle it did.

Exhausted, Kira lost consciousness in his arms, but Tristan kept a tight hold on her as Roger and the women pulled them toward the raft. Once there, Roger grabbed the teen's life jacket and pulled her onto their raft, still wedged on a boulder, by falling into a sitting position.

The girl safely in the raft, Roger was back on his knees and held out his oar, the T-grip end toward Tristan. His arms like jelly, Tristan grabbed hold and let his coworker pull him.

"We've got to get the guide," Tristan said as he toppled into the raft. Adrenaline driving him, he got to his knees and undid the rope from the girl.

"Maybe he can float down the river to a calm spot, like the others," Roger suggested.

"Let's try to get him in." Tristan signaled to the guide that he planned to toss the rope to him. At the man's nod, he found the strength to throw it.

Laura and Jenny were attending to the teen while Roger and Tristan pulled the guide to their raft. Lucia stayed at the helm, oar in hand in case they got dislodged from the boulder.

They quickly had the guide on the raft.

"Name's Steve and, man, was I glad to see you," the guide said. "Great job. Our whole raft capsized and two got stuck. I got one free and to shore, but couldn't make it to Kira—ended up losing my oar in the process of trying, and wasn't able to do much until help arrived. Thank God, you weren't far behind us."

Tristan nodded then turned to where Jenny and Laura were bent over the unconscious girl. "How is she?"

"Hypothermia and her ankle's broken," Jenny said, not looking up from where she tended to the teen. "Abrasions and one spot that needs a few stitches. The cold water kept the bleeding slowed."

Jenny lifted the towel she'd pressed to the area to reveal the wound.

"She probably got the cut when we were freeing her," Tristan admitted, hating that there hadn't been another way.

"It could have been so much worse," the guide pointed out.

What the man said was true. Assessing how their raft perched on the boulder with the water sluicing around them, Tristan calculated the best way to free them so they could get Kira further medical care.

His eyes met Jenny's and what he saw there

stole his breath as surely as if he'd plunged back into the water. Her dark eyes swirled with concern. For him.

Just a natural response given the situation, he reminded himself. What he saw meant nothing. Still, her look had him wanting to high-five the sun.

Later, he thought. Later, they'd talk. Now, they had to get moving.

"Jenny, I want you in the center to keep a hold on Kira. We only have a short section to get through before we'll be in calm waters, but we don't want to lose her out of the raft. Lucia will take your spot and Steve will move up front with Roger." He gave a reassuring smile then glanced around at the rest of the crew. "Let's get this raft to shore and call for help."

Sitting in the middle as Tristan had said, Kira positioned between her legs, Jenny kept her arms around the girl to provide as much warmth as she could as the raft bumped its way through the river to reach where they could paddle to shore. Roger and Steve jumped out and pulled the boat onto the pebbly embankment.

Once there, everyone but Jenny, Tristan and

the girl got out of the raft. Steve called for help while Tristan and Jenny tended to Kira.

"Not awake yet?"

Rubbing her palms over the girl's arms to increase circulation, Jenny shook her head. "No, but her pulse is strong and she's breathing okay."

"Good. Keep her wrapped. I'm going to check her ankle."

He knelt next to where Jenny held the girl.

"You were very brave." Jenny watched him pull a small first-aid kit from his life vest.

"It's not a big deal, just what I used to do," he said, setting about cleaning the open wounds with disinfectant.

"You could have been hurt. I was scared for you," she admitted, continuing to rub the girl's arms. Surely, Kira would wake up soon?

Tristan glanced at her and grinned. "Does that mean I'm growing on you?"

His smile held that flirtatiousness that set off warning bells. Heaven save her from gorgeous men with dimples and cleft chins.

"I hope not."

He laughed. "Well, if it would help make that happen, I'll volunteer for more water rescues."

At the thought of him back in the raging river, Jenny's stomach clenched. "Don't you dare. Lord forbid that there's need of any more water rescues."

"You're right, but it's the thought that counts." He pushed the deepest gash together and strategically placed a Steri-Strip across it, pulling the cold skin closed and then taping a piece of gauze over the area. "Do I get credit for being willing to volunteer to impress you?"

"You don't have to volunteer to impress me, Tristan. I've been impressed since the moment we met, and you know it." She sighed. "Everyone knows it."

If she'd thought his grin appealing before, this one was positively wicked.

His mouth opened and Jenny could only imagine what he'd been going to say, but he was stopped by Kira rousing and mumbling something incoherent.

"Hey, Kira. Glad to see those eyes again." Tristan smiled at the girl, but in a way that, although just as appealing, was gentle and reassuring rather than flirtatious as his smile had been with Jenny.

That she was out of the water hit, and Kira burst into tears.

"Shh. It's okay," Jenny soothed, hugging the girl.

"Your ankle is broken, and you've got a cut that'll need sutures, but help is on the way and you're going to be okay."

Seeing that the girl was awake, Steve came over. "We're not that far off the main road, so help should be here soon."

"That's good news, isn't it, Kira?" Jenny said to the girl, holding her close.

"Everyone from our raft is accounted for and fine," Steve noted. "As a matter of fact, here come two of them now. That's your parents making their way down the bank."

Sure enough, the two who had made it to shore were now just a few yards away where they'd taken off on land in the direction the raft had been floating.

From that moment, everything happened fast. A rescue unit arrived and took over. Steve profusely thanked their group for their heroics, as did the others from the overturned raft. A few snapped photos of Tristan. He shook off their claims of heroism, seeming embarrassed by the attention, and saying it had been a team effort.

As they were no longer needed, and with a lot of dread on Jenny's part, they set back off in their raft.

"What happened with Steve's raft is a one-off. Just remember, if you go out, toes up at all times," Tristan reiterated.

Jenny pushed her toes as far as she could beneath the seat in front of her, wedging them into the rubbery crevice. Having been reminded of the dangers lurking beneath the water's surface, her initial fear was back rather than the happy adrenaline she'd felt earlier as they'd ridden wave after wave. The last thing she wanted was to go overboard.

They paddled for an hour prior to stopping at where they'd have lunch.

"You're tight as a drum," Tristan pointed out once they exited the boat. Laura had snuck off for a bathroom break and Roger and Lucia had moved to a grassy area up on the embankment for a semiprivate picnic.

Lingering next to where he pulled items from the raft, Jenny shrugged. "I keep thinking about Kira."

"She'll be okay. It'll take her a while, but she's young and should fully recover."

Jenny trembled. "You saved her. I was so scared for her, and you knew just what to do."

"If we hadn't come along, someone else would have," he said, his voice calm, soothing. "All the guides are trained for rescue. Any of them would have done what I did. Probably better than I did."

Jenny wasn't having his modesty. She'd witnessed what he'd done, how fearlessly he'd jumped to action with little thought to his own safety. "I thought you were wonderful."

"There you go making me want to look for volunteer opportunities." He grinned. "Seriously, as much as I appreciate your praise, it wasn't a big deal."

"It was to Kira and her family. To Steve, too. He felt terrible about what happened although, from the sounds of things, he couldn't have prevented it."

"No guide wants someone to get hurt during their watch."

"The Colorado River lost a great guide when you started nursing school."

At her praise, Tristan's gaze shot to hers, as blue as the sky above them.

"But I'm glad it did," she continued, "because you're a wonderful nurse and our patients are lucky to have you caring for them." She paused, took a deep breath. "As difficult as I find admitting it, knowing you makes me lucky, too."

Standing, he stared down at her, his eyes searching hers. Although, for what, she wasn't sure, just knowing that whatever it was, she didn't think she was strong enough to deny him anything he wished.

"Jenny, I—"

"Phew, I feel lots better," Laura announced, joining them and then spraying her hands with the sanitizer. "And will feel even better after we have a bite to eat. Anything water-related makes me so hungry."

Wanting to grasp hold of his arm to stay him from turning away, wondering what he'd been going to say, Jenny held her breath, hoping he'd continue, but knew the moment had been lost.

After one last look, Tristan pulled out the waterproof bag that held their lunch. He tossed a granola bar and sandwich to Laura, then handed Jenny hers.

"Eat up. We've still got a few hours on the river."

Jenny grabbed her water bottle then found a place along the bank to sit to watch the water while she ate. Hard to believe the sunshine-dappled river that appeared so peaceful had not so long ago loomed dark and dangerous.

"It really is beautiful here," Laura said, sitting beside her. "I'm sorry your first trip had drama. I've never seen a rescue, much less participated in one. Most of the time folks fall out of the boat and just float to the next slow spot, then get pulled back up into the raft. No big deal."

Jenny wasn't sure about that.

"Steve seemed like a nice guy," Laura continued, taking a bite of her sandwich.

Jenny's eyes widened. "Is that why you were all smiles with him while we were waiting on the ambulance? Because he was a 'nice guy'?"

Laura grinned. "Something like that. I got his phone number."

Jenny shook her head. "I can't believe you picked up a guy."

"Hey, nice guys are difficult to find."

"So difficult that you met one while floating down the river."

Laura gave a so-sue-me shrug. "If you have

half a brain, you'll quit fighting the attraction between you and Tristan and pick him up, too."

"I already have his number and it's not one I should call."

Laura rolled her eyes. "The man saved a girl's life. The least he deserves is a hero's kiss."

She wanted to kiss him. When they'd been standing there, she'd wanted him to take her into his arms and kiss her. What had he been going to say?

But she wasn't ready to share that with Laura. "Your new guide friend might not appreciate you doing that."

Unfazed, Laura shrugged. "Then I guess it'll have to be you who gives Tristan a kiss for being so brave."

A shower had never felt so good. Jenny let the lukewarm water rush over her body. The spray wasn't particularly strong but washing away the river in the tiny stall of the campground's shower house was heavenly. She lathered her hair, rinsed and conditioned. Oh, yeah, this was heavenly.

The remainder of their rafting trip had been uneventful.

If you could call being more and more drawn to Tristan uneventful.

What was it about him that appealed so much? Yes, he was gorgeous, but she'd met more traditionally handsome men. Yet none appealed the way he did. Not even Geoffrey or Carlos. *It's his eyes*, she thought. How when he smiled, his eyes smiled, too. Or maybe it was just the smile in general. He had a great smile and he wielded it often. Where most of the men she knew wielded arrogance as a second skin, Tristan didn't seem that way at all. When Roger had been telling the others from their group what had happened, Tristan had yet again downplayed his role, citing that the rescue couldn't have happened without a team effort.

Jenny rinsed then towel dried her body, knowing her muscles should feel achy from the strenuous river trek, but instead feeling revitalized.

Feeling alive and good and…feminine.

The river water had obviously gone to her head and clouded her mind. Maybe some type of parasite had invaded her and was making her have the thoughts she'd been having all afternoon. Thoughts no doubt triggered by her bestie's crazy suggestions. Kiss Tristan. Was Laura insane?

Dressed in black leggings and a Rock City T-shirt, hair still wet but combed through, Jenny made her way back to their campsite.

The first person she saw was Tristan. Like her, his hair was damp from his recent shower. Wearing shorts, a T-shirt and comfy-appearing sandals, he looked completely relaxed as he took a sip of his drink then laughed at something someone said. He turned, their glances met, and her lips curved upward of their own accord. That had to be it, because her brain knew better than to smile at him just because he'd grinned at seeing her.

Heart pounding, she closed the distance to where he stood with her friends.

"Better?" he asked when she joined him, Laura, Roger and Lucia where they chatted near Tristan's 4Runner.

"Much," she admitted, still smiling and trying not to berate her silly mouth for its traitorous actions. "I'm also starved. Something smells amazing."

"Burgers are on the grill. There are drinks in the cooler. Help yourself."

Jenny lifted the lid, bypassed the alcoholic options, and grabbed a water. Her friends had pulled chairs over, but Tristan sat on the back of his open hatch.

"Have a seat," he offered, patting to the spot next to him.

She'd been in the raft with him all day, but for some reason, sitting next to him on the SUV seemed intimate, as if she were pairing off with him. And despite the tumultuous thoughts playing through her mind, she wasn't ready to publicly do that. "I should help with dinner."

"We all tried," Laura proclaimed, Roger and Lucia nodding their agreement.

"Blake and his wife refuse to let anyone near the grill, saying cooking dinner is their treat. Based on the way it smells, they've got things under control." Tristan's attention still connected to her, he took another sip. "Plus, there's only so much room by the grill. Stay."

"I… Okay. I'll put my bag in the tent and be right back." She tossed her toiletries into the tent she shared with Laura then, needing a moment, climbed in and ran her fingers through her damp hair again and started plaiting it into a single long braid. Sitting with her friends before a meal was no big deal.

But when she returned to where Tristan still sat on the open hatch of his 4Runner, he was alone.

"Where are the others?"

"Laura got a call. Roger and Lucia said something about going for a walk." He shrugged. "Looks as if it's just you and me until they get back."

It wouldn't surprise her if they didn't return but had purposely left her with Tristan. She sat across from him in Laura's vacated chair.

Not seeming surprised that she'd not chosen to sit beside him, Tristan lifted his drink in a salute.

Why had she sat at all? Jenny wondered moments later when they were still sitting in silence just looking at one another. She couldn't say it was a completely awkward silence, but it wasn't comfortable, either.

It was…disturbingly exhilarating.

"Barring what happened to Kira, I enjoyed today." She was chatting, not to fill the silence between her and Tristan, but to block her own thoughts.

"Once you relaxed and gave it a chance," he

pointed out. "I love the thrill of riding down the river."

"It showed. Thank you for keeping us all safe."

"You keep giving me credit where credit isn't due, but I'll take it."

"I figured you would," she teased. Then, watching the sway of his feet where they hung off the end of his SUV, she asked, "So now what do we do?"

He shrugged. "Sit, eat, drink, be merry while enjoying each other's company and being out in nature."

"And not being at work," she added.

"There's that, but I love being a nurse."

"It shows. I meant what I said earlier. Your patients are lucky to have you. You're a great nurse, Tristan. One of the best travel nurses we've ever had."

His eyes twinkled. "You keep complimenting me and I'm going to get a big head."

She doubted it but smiled. "Fine. You're terrible. I hate it when I'm assigned to work with you. I..." She paused because she had hated it, hadn't she?

Only, not really. She'd just wanted to hate it.

Instead, as much as she'd denied it, she'd been

drawn to him as surely as a moth to a flame, moving purely on instinct when what should have been happening was that instinct telling her to get out of Dodge before she got burned.

"Laura's phone call was from Steve. She'd invited him to hang with us tonight. From the sound of it, he was on his way and needed directions to our campsite."

"To hang out with her, you mean?" Jenny asked, grateful he'd changed the subject. "She mentioned that she'd gotten his phone number. If he called, then he must have gotten hers, too."

"Either that or she texted him, letting him know she was serious with her invitation and giving him the chance to decide if he was interested."

Jenny nodded. "That's probably what she did."

"He asked me about her after we were all ashore—if she was single. I mentioned it to her. I guess she's keen on him because, within minutes, she had his number and was inviting him for burgers tonight."

"That's great. I hope they hit it off." Mostly, she did, although she worried about her friend getting hurt when it didn't work out. After all, how could it when they didn't live or work anywhere near each other?

"Me, too," Tristan admitted then added, "I'll admit that when he pulled me aside, I was grateful he wasn't interested in you."

Eyes wide, Jenny's gaze shot to his.

"I owe you an apology because I told him you were taken before he even got a chance to say who he liked. I didn't want to risk it."

She let what he was admitting digest.

"Does it upset you that I told him you weren't available?"

She shook her head. "No. I'm not interested in Steve."

"But you are interested in someone?"

Jenny took a deep breath. She was. Him. Out in the woods, real life seemed far away and, letting herself fantasize that she could look him in the eyes and tell him that she liked him, that she'd wanted to throw her arms around him and kiss him at several points during the day, didn't seem nearly so farfetched. And yet, still she hesitated.

"Jenny?" he prompted. "Are you interested in someone? In me?"

A movement beyond his vehicle caught her

attention and she leapt to her feet. “Oh, there’s Laura now. I should ask her about the phone call with Steve.”

Behind her, Tristan laughed. “Running away, Jenny?”

“As fast as I can,” she called over her shoulder as she made her way to Laura.

But she suspected her feet couldn’t move nearly quick enough to keep her from being caught.

CHAPTER SEVEN

"MARSHMALLOW?" TRISTAN WAVED the bag in front of Jenny. Their eyes had been playing games all evening. Hers making contact, sometimes looking away, sometimes studying him for long moments, as if trying to figure him out.

"Sure." She smiled up at him. "Why not have a big fluff of sticky sugar?"

"Especially when it's melted and sandwiched between chocolate and graham crackers." He waggled his brows and extended his arm to help her from her chair.

"Exactly." Jenny eyed his hand and he thought she'd stand without taking it, but with a sharp intake of breath, she placed hers in his and let him help her to her feet.

Within his, her hand was warm, small, almost fragile. Yet he knew exactly how capable it was; that she worked hard and used those hands to care for her patients shift after shift.

Her eyes dropped to their hands then glanced

up at him with questions in her gaze. Before he could say anything, she pulled free. "Thanks."

Moving to a vacant chair close to the fire, she speared her marshmallow prior to extending it above the fire so the confection could melt.

"Slow and steady," Tristan observed from where he watched her hold the white puff above the flames.

"Pardon?"

"You roast your marshmallow with a great deal of patience, letting it slowly melt rather than burn to an impatient crisp."

"I like the gooey inside but not the black outside, like Roger and Lucia were making theirs last night. Not that I've had the chance to do this often. Just once at a church gathering," she admitted, smiling at him. "But I recall that I didn't like it burned."

"Then you may want to move that," he suggested, gesturing to her marshmallow that had caught fire.

"Oh!" She jerked back on the roasting stick. Unfortunately, the flaming marshmallow had softened so, when she yanked, a hot glob flung straight toward her.

Tristan flipped the bag he held in front of her

and the marshmallow smacked against it. Dropping the bag, he put out the fire with his shoe, kicking the remainder of the debris-covered confection into the fire pit.

"I'm so sorry," Jenny moaned. "Your shoe is going to be a mess."

Probably, but it would clean.

"I'm just glad it didn't hit you." His body had seemed to move in slow motion when he'd realized what was happening. He'd never have forgiven himself if he'd let her hurt herself doing something he'd suggested.

"Thanks to you, I'm fine," she noted, but her eyes dropped to his hand. "But some did splatter onto you." She winced. "If I'd been thinking, I'd have known better than to do something so stupid. Sometimes I'm such a klutz."

The burn registered about the time she pointed out where the tiny white glob stuck to the back of his hand. He'd been so worried the marshmallow was going to hit her that he hadn't noticed.

"You're not a klutz. It's not a big deal. I have burn cream in my first-aid kit," he assured, carefully removing the sticky glob from his sensitized skin. The area stung but was less than a centimeter in diameter. "I'll be fine."

Going with him to his SUV, she popped open the cooler next to his truck and scooped out a piece of ice. The sloshing of the ice against the side of the cup she used seemed to match the throb of his burn as he dug out the first-aid kit.

Once he'd settled onto the back of the SUV, Jenny took his hand and placed the ice on the burned spot. "It's my fault you got burned. I feel terrible."

Having her touch him was worth enduring much worse than the minor burn. For that matter, where she held his hand to steady it so she could press the ice to the injured skin burned much more than the marshmallow had.

"Obviously, we now know that I can't be trusted with a flaming marshmallow," she mumbled as she kept the melting ice to his wound.

"The nursing care that follows more than makes up for your lack of marshmallow skills, but in the future, I'll roast them for you."

Her gaze lifted to his. Swallowing, she loosened her grip on his hand, but kept the ice in place over his burn.

Her fingers shook. "What exactly is it you want from me, Tristan?"

Great question. And one he didn't know the

complete answer to. For the moment, looking into her big eyes, the reflection of the moonlight dancing in their depths, he knew exactly what he wanted. He wanted to kiss her, to taste the fullness of her parted lips, to feel her against him.

But he suspected if he said those things out loud, she'd retreat into her tent, possibly not to make an appearance until it was time to leave. Still, he wouldn't lie to her.

"I've not made it a secret that I'm attracted to you and would like to know you better while I'm in Chattanooga."

Taking a deep breath, she glanced down to where she pressed the ice. "You seem to be a great guy, Tristan, but you and I would never work. You have to know that."

"Because I'm only here for a few months?"

"That, but mostly because of Sawyer."

Tristan's stomach twisted. When he'd asked Laura if Jenny was dating anyone, her friend had laughed, shaken her head, and told him to go for it. Had she been setting him up for failure or trying to interfere with a bad relationship she didn't approve of?

"Who's Sawyer?" Why was his heart racing so at his question?

Although obviously emotionally torn, she smiled, and there was no doubt it was a real one. Whoever Sawyer was, Jenny was hooked.

"My four-year-old son. He's my whole world."

Tristan's jaw dropped. Jenny had a kid?

"I didn't know you were a mom." Some of the things that had been said at the hospital clicked into place. Had everyone just assumed he'd known and so had never felt the need to say anything?

Jenny gave him an odd look. "I'm not sure how you didn't. I talk about him a lot at the hospital."

"You've not exactly been the mecca of conversation with me since I arrived," he reminded her, still trying to process that she was a mother. "Quite the opposite."

"True, but I didn't purposely try to keep you from knowing about Sawyer. He's the best part of my life."

Tristan mused on that. Jenny had a son.

"But I was trying my best to keep away from you. You scare me."

"Me?" he asked, shocked that she'd made such a revealing admission. "I've never seen myself as scary. More like the goofy guy next door who is friends with everyone."

"You've obviously never seen yourself through a woman who doesn't want to get hurt's eyes. Believe me, you're scary."

Her admission gutted him, made him want to go all white knight to whomever had hurt her and made her so cautious.

"Sometimes facing our fears is the best way to get over them. Just look at how you overcame your fear of the river today and ended up having a good time, despite a few ups and downs."

What was he saying? Better yet, why was he saying it? He didn't typically date coworkers or women with kids. Jenny was both. He should steer well clear. Instead, he clung to the fact that she still held his hand and that her touch singed his flesh much more than the gooey marshmallow.

She also held his interest. More so than any woman in recent history. Maybe ever, as he sure couldn't think of anyone who'd affected him the way she did.

"You may be right about that. And, if it was just me that I had to look out for, maybe I would be brave enough to do just that, but it's not just me. I have Sawyer to consider." She took a deep breath then stared directly into his eyes. "No matter how much I'm attracted to you, and it's no secret that I am, I'm not interested in bringing a man into my and Sawyer's lives who won't be here more than a few months. Letting Sawyer get close to someone who isn't going to stick around wouldn't be fair."

What she said made perfect sense.

"I get that, and on some level, even agree," he admitted. "I don't want to hurt you or your son. Maybe we can be friends."

She half laughed. "Do you really believe that's possible?" Her tone said she didn't.

"I'm not sure, but I do know that the most exciting part of this weekend is that you're here, and that the moment you touched my hand, the only burn I felt was where our skin touched. Maybe you're right and that means just being friends won't be easy when I want more, but I'm willing to try if you are."

Although she kept the ice in place, she immediately released her hold of his hand. "I—I'm not sure what to say."

He shrugged. "There's no rule that says you have to say anything."

"Yet I feel as if I'm supposed to say something. Not doing so just feels awkward."

"My intention isn't to make you feel awkward, but I get the impression that you do feel uncomfortable around me."

"Of course, I do. You're scary, remember?"

"We really need to work on that. Tell me, Jenny, what is it you find the scariest about me?"

Her forehead creased.

"Don't worry about the big picture of my scariness. Just tell me what scares you right now in this moment?"

She swallowed, closed her eyes and asked, "The scariest thing about you at this very moment?"

He nodded.

"That once upon a time I'd have jumped at the chance of spending time with you, having sex with you." She took a deep breath. "Even knowing you'd leave me. Now...well, I've learned from past mistakes and have to make better choices. You aren't a good choice. I won't have Sawyer hurt."

She said her son's name, but her own pain shone on her face. Who had hurt her? Someone had. Her defensive posture triggered a swirl of emotions within him. Most of which didn't make sense. Protectiveness. That one he got. He liked taking care of people, wanted to help them heal. It was a trait he believed made him a better nurse. But it was more than just protectiveness. There was this strong urge to prove her wrong, to convince her that he was a good choice, that getting to know him would be the best decision she could ever make.

A smart man would ignore what he saw in her eyes, what he felt every time they were near each other, and just take her at her word. A smart man wouldn't point out the vulnerability in her eyes demanded he do something to heal the gaping wounds another lover had caused.

He was no knight in shining armor. It wasn't his place or desire to do anything beyond being friendly with his coworkers. And yet he couldn't walk away.

"This isn't as complicated as you're making it. We're each intrigued by the other, but we are in agreement that a romantic relationship is out of the question. Why can't we just enjoy each other's company, at least for the rest of the weekend, no sex necessary?"

Yeah right, on the "no sex necessary." Jenny wasn't buying it. Men had been saying that to women since the beginning of time so they'd lower their guard and their pants. Why else would Tristan want to spend time "getting to know" her when he'd soon leave if not because of physical chemistry? That, they had in spades. Gigantic bunches. Explosive chemistry that made her want to rip off his clothes and kiss him from head to toe.

She wished it wasn't so, but just making eye contact with him put her off kilter in ways no man ever had. Tristan had some major pheromones going and they were making her insides dance to a crazy tune.

"Come on, Jenny. Letting go to enjoy the rest of the weekend together shouldn't be such a difficult decision to make. It's not as if I'm asking you to marry me."

Jenny flinched. Ouch. His comment shouldn't have stung, but it did. Tristan wanting to marry her hadn't crossed her mind. And yet, foolishly, she did feel hurt, as if he were somehow implying she wasn't good enough to marry.

Or perhaps Geoffrey's taunts had come back to haunt her? Not that Geoffrey had been free to marry her since he'd already been engaged, but at the time Jenny hadn't known that. She'd just known that an amazingly handsome and charismatic doctor had swept her off her still-in-nursing-school feet, promised her his undying love and, like the naïve twenty-year-old she'd been, she'd believed him.

For all she knew, Tristan had a fiancée or even a wife and kids somewhere.

Why did the thought cause a fresh wave of pain? Swallowing the sob that wanted to escape, she took a deep breath instead and gestured to Tristan's burn. "Is the ice helping?"

He let out a frustrated noise. "I guess that means you're finished talking about us?"

"There is no 'us.'" Her words sounded more confident than she felt, which strengthened her to continue on the offensive. "You're a great-looking man, Tristan, not to mention smart and funny, and a genuinely nice guy. I imagine lots of women are attracted to you. You'd be much better off spending your time pursuing one of them. I'm not worth the trouble. I have a kid." Hadn't Carlos implied that made her unworthy of his love?

"You're worth the trouble, Jenny. Give me this weekend to show you."

Frustrated, she pushed against his chest. "I'm not sleeping with you, Tristan."

"That's not what I'm asking you to do. I'll be here for less than three months and, if you ever have a relationship again, you need it to be more than a short-term one. Fine. Let's just enjoy being together with no pressure for anything more instead of throwing walls up between the attraction we feel for each other."

"Walls aren't a bad thing."

"In certain scenarios, I'm sure you're right, but in this case they're not good. You don't need walls around me, Jenny. I'm not going to hurt you."

"You can't guarantee that you won't hurt me."

He hesitated. "No, I guess not. But we both know where the other one stands. That I'm leaving soon and there wouldn't be anything permanent between us. Let me be the opportunity for you to be reminded of how much fun life is."

Life was fun. She had fun when she read Sawyer a story, when they went to the park and she pushed him as high as he'd go on the swings with him begging her to go even higher, when they played games and he'd giggle incessantly when he beat her. When… She paused. All the fun moments flooding her were tied to Sawyer. Not a single one was something revolving around her own life other than as his mother.

Part of her didn't mind. She loved being Sawyer's mother. But another part, the part that screamed to her that she was only twenty-five years old, was young, and healthy, and that it wasn't wrong to be attracted to a beautiful man...well, that part minded.

What Tristan said was as hopeless as it was tempting.

"How do I magically make the way I feel disappear? How do I lower those walls when it's easier to leave them up and not worry about getting hurt or having Sawyer hurt?"

The glow from the moonlight flickered in his eyes, dancing with a mesmerizing rhythm that lured her further under his spell. "Promise you won't be mad and I'll tell you."

She sighed. "Please don't say that my sleeping with you would make the awkwardness go away, because we both know that would only make things worse."

"I don't know that, but that wasn't what I was going to say. Close, though."

"What?"

"Not sex, but we need to kiss."

Jenny rolled her eyes. "Of course, you think that."

"Hear me out. What if there's all this sexual tension between us and one kiss would dissipate it? If one kiss could put you at ease to where you could treat me no different from any other travel nurse doing a rotation at the hospital? If what you say is true, that you don't want a relationship with me during the time I'm here, getting rid of the attraction would be the perfect solution."

Jenny considered what he was saying. As much as she thought he was just wanting to make out, maybe he was onto something. If he was a bad kisser, then she'd be grossed out and whatever it was that lit up inside her when he was near would stop and he'd be just another guy, like Roger, and maybe this tension inside her would subside and they could be friends. Or at least coworkers, rather than her feeling all fluttery inside.

Or maybe she was just tired of fighting what she felt, what she saw in his eyes. Maybe, despite all her protests and reasons why she shouldn't, she really did want to throw caution to the wind and cling to any reason to kiss him.

Maybe she wanted to kiss her completely-wrong-for-her frog despite knowing he'd never morph into her Prince Charming.

Aware that no one could see them where his SUV was parked, Jenny acted purely on gut instinct, stood on her tippy toes and pressed her mouth to Tristan's.

Jenny's mouth was warm, soft, *fragile*. Like a delicate butterfly's wing brushing against Tristan's lips. He suspected if he applied the slightest pressure she'd fly away. Even though he longed to deepen their kiss, he stood still, keeping his hands to his sides and ordering himself to be content with her lips touching his.

In the moonlight, he could see her closed eyes, could see the uncertainty on her face, could feel her body quiver. Or was that his body? He wasn't sure. He just knew that kissing Jenny wasn't going to make the ache inside him go away, but rather intensify his reaction every time she was near.

He hadn't thought it would. Not really. But it had been worth a shot when she'd been so adamant that they couldn't be together. He should be the one being adamant. Instead, he was shaking like a teenaged boy receiving his first kiss.

His gaze never leaving her, he watched the play of emotions the moonlight lit across her face. He'd never expected Jenny to take his suggestion seriously. That she had had blown him away. That her mouth pressed against his blew him away.

It took all his willpower to let her pull back, knowing that she might never allow him this close again, that he might never breathe her breath or feel the warmth of her body again, but he managed, somehow. If only there was more light so he could read everything her now-open eyes revealed as she stared at him. Awe, wonder, curiosity, regret? He couldn't be sure, he just knew emotions were high.

Afraid he'd say the wrong thing if he opened his mouth, he waited so he could take his cue from her. But she didn't say anything, just seemed to be registering what she'd done.

Please don't regret this, he mentally ordered. *Please give us a chance.*

A chance for what? he wondered. He didn't allow that curiosity to take hold, just lived in the moment, prepared for Jenny to push him away when what he wanted was to hold her tight. Just when he thought she was going to retreat, she pressed her lips to his again, this time with more pressure, more exploration, and as much as he didn't want to crush her fragility, he kissed her back.

Still, the kiss was more sweet than passionate. More tasting, exploring, than consuming, but it wouldn't take much for him to fully ignite and go up in flames. Her touch was that powerful, he was that receptive to what was happening.

A bit breathy, she pulled back and stared up at him, her eyes full of wonder and concern. "That just brought things to a whole new level of awkward."

"Bad?" he asked, willing her to admit that it hadn't been, that she'd felt the magic of their complicated touch.

She shook her head.

Hope blossomed. "Good?"

After a moment's hesitation, she sighed. "You already know you're a great kisser. To even suggest that our kissing would make this…whatever this is between us…go away was ludicrous. You tricked me and now I need to think about this."

"I wasn't trying to trick you. It could have

worked." He touched her face, brushing his thumb across the softness of her cheek. "Don't overthink what happened, Jenny. You'll drive yourself crazy and it accomplishes nothing."

"All the same, I do need to think about what just happened." She took a few steps back. "Everyone will be heading to their tents since we have to be up early."

He could feel the walls going up. Frustration hit at how much he wanted to claw them down into such rubble that she couldn't ever hide behind them again.

"Jenny?"

She paused.

"In case you were wondering, had you asked me about our kiss, my answer would be good. Very, very good."

CHAPTER EIGHT

"YOU LEFT THIS in my vehicle."

Wiping the sleep from her eyes, Jenny stared at the man standing on her front porch. Was she dreaming? She'd gone from seeing him with her eyes closed to waking from her doorbell ringing and finding him freshly showered, wearing jeans and a navy T-shirt, standing on her front porch.

"Tristan? What are you doing here?" That he held her hat in his hands registered. "You didn't need to bring that to me. I mean, you could have brought it to work this evening. That would have been fine."

"Bringing it by wasn't a big deal and this way you don't have to worry about keeping track of it at work."

"Thank you." She took the hat from him, saw her mother's car pulling into the drive, and felt a moment of panic. Could she just make Tristan disappear so that her mother and Sawyer didn't see him?

But even as she thought it, Tristan turned to see who she was looking at, and Jenny faced the inevitable. Sawyer and her mother were about to meet Tristan. The man she'd kissed and wanted to do so much more with. She hadn't, though. She'd kissed him and walked away because he was no frog prince.

Sighing, Jenny brushed past him to help her mother.

"Hi, Mom," she said as her mother's car door opened. "How was your weekend?"

"I was just about to ask you the same." Her mother motioned to where Tristan stood on the porch. "From the look of things, I'm guessing things went well."

Was she implying that Tristan had stayed the night? Jenny gawked at her mother's knowing look.

"I left my hat in Tristan's vehicle this morning when he dropped me off." There, she'd let her mother know that he hadn't stayed the night. "He found it and was just dropping it by. He just got here."

"Tristan. I've not heard you mention him. He's who you went camping with?" her mother asked, obviously intrigued.

"I went with a whole group from work. Tristan just happened to be who Laura and I rode with to the Ocoee." Her friend should have been with her on the way back home, but had bailed, choosing to ride with Roger and Lucia. "It's not a big deal." Hoping her mother didn't see right through her and somehow know Jenny had kissed him, she opened Sawyer's door. "Hey, you. Did you have a great weekend with Grammy in Gatlinburg?"

Grinning, Sawyer nodded as she undid his safety seat. "Eli and I slept under the shark tanks. You have to go do that, Mom. They were huge. You'd love it."

Jenny smiled at her world. "Sounds as if you loved it. I sure missed you."

His blond head bobbed up and down as he climbed out of the car. The moment his feet were on the ground, Jenny wrapped him in a hug.

"I see you have a new friend with you. Did Grammy get you that?"

"Grammy let me pick any stuffed animal I wanted. I started to get a shark. That's what Eli got. But then I saw him." He held up a stuffed sea turtle, but his attention moved beyond her. "Who's that man?"

"A friend from work," she answered, her cheeks flushing as she realized Tristan was walking toward them rather than waiting on the porch. Not that waiting would have helped since her mom and Sawyer would have to walk right past. *Say goodbye and leave*, she willed, but of course that wasn't what he did.

Tristan gave one of those eye-sparkling smiles. "I'm Tristan. I'm a nurse at the hospital with your mom. You must be Sawyer."

"I am." His good manners kicking in, Sawyer stuck out his hand in the most adorable way. "Nice to meet you."

Jenny's heart melted. How could he look so big and so tiny all at the same time? And why was her heart thudding so hard at his meeting Tristan?

Tristan's glimpse shot to Jenny and he grinned before returning his attention to Sawyer. "Did I hear you say something about sleeping under a shark tank?"

Sawyer nodded. "There were sharks everywhere."

Tristan's eyes widened with overexaggeration. "Was that at the aquarium? It sounds really cool."

Excitement filling his eyes, Sawyer nodded. "I went with Grammy and Giles and Eli to Gatlinburg. Sharks were swimming around us all night."

"Weren't you scared?"

"No." Sawyer giggled. "They were in a tank."

"That's good." Tristan bent to Sawyer's level. "Who's your friend?"

"This is my sea turtle. I named him Freddie, but that's not what the sea turtle at the Chattanooga aquarium's name is. There are two sea turtles there." Sawyer talked a mile a minute, showing Tristan his stuffed turtle. "I like sea turtles."

"The kid likes anything that's in the water," Jenny's mom interjected with what Jenny could only describe as a delighted giggle. "I'm Geneva, by the way. So, you and Jenny work together?"

Oh, Mom, please don't.

"For a short while. I'm a travel nurse and only here for a few months."

"Travel nursing? That sounds adventurous." Her mother popped the car trunk. "Sawyer, be a dear and grab your things."

"Can I help carry something?" Tristan offered, earning major brownie points from Jenny's mother.

Her eyes lit up. "Would you mind? That would be wonderful."

And that was how Tristan ended up inside their house and invited to stay for a late lunch.

"If I'd known we were going to have company, I'd have had something ready, but we're sure glad you came by today anyway," Geneva told him while pouring Tristan a glass of sweet tea.

"He's not here to socialize, Mom, just to drop off my hat."

"That doesn't mean we shouldn't feed him. He might be hungry."

Her mother had no idea.

Jenny wavered between wanting to smack her own head with her palm and being amused at how her mother carried on. You'd have thought Jenny had never brought a man home. Then again, there hadn't been many. A few in high school and her early university days, then Geoffrey after she'd started nursing school, and Carlos a few years ago.

"No problem, ma'am," Tristan assured her. "But Jenny's right. I just stopped by to bring her hat. She left it when I dropped her off this morning."

"That's what she said earlier." Had her mother not believed her? "So, y'all had a great trip?"

"I did," Tristan confirmed. "I'm not sure we'll convince Jenny to go rafting again, though."

"Oh?"

"Tristan had to rescue a girl who was stuck in the river."

"Under the water?"

"Just her foot was wedged under a rock."

Sawyer swam his turtle through the air. "If Freddie had been there, he could have freed her."

"Freddie would have come in handy," Tristan quipped.

"That reminds me," Jenny mused. "I need to check to see if you got into the next session for swimming lessons."

The timing of the previous session hadn't worked for her work schedule, but after this weekend, now more than ever, she wanted Sawyer to know how to swim.

His big eyes met hers. "Can Freddie go, too?"

"You think Freddie can offer some tips?" Jenny asked, reaching for her cellular phone. "If so, then I'm all for it. Excuse me while I pull up my email. Sawyer has been on a wait list for the next session, and I'll need to confirm quickly as I don't want to miss getting him in."

Unfortunately, the email said that the remainder of the summer sessions were full but they'd notify her if there were any cancellations.

"Everything okay?"

Jenny shrugged. "Just frustrated that Sawyer's still on a wait list. I'd hoped he'd learn to swim this summer, but short of finding someone to give private lessons, that may not happen."

"I can teach him."

Jenny blinked. "You?"

"Sure. I'm a trained lifeguard and there's a pool at the apartment complex where I'm staying. With Freddie's help, teaching Sawyer would be a breeze."

Sawyer's eyes were huge, pleading. "Can I, Mom?"

How could she say no? If she let her attraction to Tristan get in the way of Sawyer learning to swim and something happened, she'd never forgive herself.

"Oh, that's wonderful, Tristan," Jenny's mother praised, clasping her hands together and eyeing him as if he were the greatest thing ever. "Sawyer needs to know how to swim and what better way than being taught by a friend?"

Jenny could think of several dozen, but she had to do what was best for Sawyer. What was best for her son was making sure he learned to swim.

"I… Mom's right. That would be great. Thank you."

"Yay! Did you hear that, Freddie? I'm going to learn to swim!" Sawyer jumped around, the turtle snug in his arms. "Can we start today?"

Tristan shrugged. "I don't have to be anywhere until work tonight."

"Don't you have something you need to be doing? Sleeping, maybe?" Because Jenny needed time to assimilate that Tristan would be teaching Sawyer to swim.

He shook his head. "With sleeping last night, I'll take a short nap before going into work, but otherwise, I'm free."

Sawyer continued to bounce with excitement. "Can we please, Mama? Freddie likes swimming."

"Freddie, eh?" She sighed, not seeing a way around saying yes. "Fine. If Mr. Scott is okay with giving you a swimming lesson, then we can go for a quick one today."

"Yay!" Sawyer danced around the room. "Freddie and I are going swimming."

Jenny's mom beamed at Tristan. "You saved a life this weekend and now you may save another."

"Mom!"

"Well, it's true," her mother insisted. "One never knows when knowing how to swim will be needed. Sawyer might save a life one day that will have been made possible by Tristan's generosity. Kudos to him for being so generous with his time."

What her mother said was an echo of her earlier thoughts, so she knew she was fighting a losing battle to say anything else in protest. Instead, she met Tristan's gaze. "I really do hope we aren't keeping you from something."

Taking a drink of the sweet tea her mother had insisted he have, Tristan smiled. "My laundry and I appreciate that more than you know."

"Understood." Why was Jenny smiling back as if her mother wasn't watching?

"Will you jump into the water?" Tristan asked the boy. He wasn't sure if offering to teach Jenny's son to swim was overall a good idea or not, but he'd taken training years ago, upped his lifeguard certification when he'd worked in Colorado, and helping a kid learn to swim was the right thing to do.

"Is it over my head?" Sawyer asked, looking and sounding nervous despite his earlier enthusiasm.

Tristan shook his head. "I'm standing, not swimming, so it's not over your head. Jump and I'll catch you."

Sawyer's eyes widened. "You can catch me? You're sure?"

"I'm sure I can."

"Sawyer, why don't I hold Freddie while you take your swimming lesson," Jenny suggested from where she sat on the edge of the pool, her long legs dangling in the water. He spied blue straps tied around her neck, but she wore a baggy T-shirt and shorts over them. Just as well. Her toned legs were enough of a distraction. Everything about the woman distracted him.

Sawyer gripped his turtle tighter. "Freddie likes the water."

"He does," Jenny agreed. "But I sure would like him to keep me company while you and Mr. Scott are doing your lesson."

"Tristan," he corrected. "Call me Tristan."

"Mr. Tristan," she countered, her attention staying on Sawyer.

"Better than Mr. Scott," he conceded then turned back to the boy. "Freddie would be great company for your mom while we're in the water. Moms sometimes get nervous during swim lessons."

Hesitantly, Sawyer handed over the stuffed turtle. "I guess Freddie could stay with her. He is great company."

Jenny watched Tristan try to convince Sawyer to jump into the water. The kid was usually gung-ho on everything, so to see him hesitant made her heart hurt. Did he sense her fear? Her nervousness for him?

Not that she thought Tristan would let anything happen to him, but accidents happened. Just like the girl who'd had to be rescued the day before. Not that there were any rocks or rapids in the apartment complex's pool, but still, Jenny's belly was all quivery.

"Okay, kiddo, today we are just going to do the basics, get you used to the water, and have a little fun. You ready?"

Standing on the side of the pool next to her, Sawyer nodded.

"We can hold off on you jumping into the water for later," he wisely suggested, earning a look of relief from Sawyer. "For now, let's get you in the water for your first superhero lesson."

Sawyer's eyes widened. "Superhero lesson?"

"Yep. First, there are some superhero rules that you should know."

From where he stood at the edge of the pool, Sawyer hung on to Tristan's every word.

"Rule number one. At no point will a superhero be forced to do anything he or she doesn't want to do."

Sawyer nodded.

"Second rule—" Tristan held up two fingers "—is that superheroes have to trust their teacher completely and have faith in the knowledge that their methods will develop the superhero's own superpowers. A superhero must listen closely and do exactly as their teacher instructs. Self-doubt is a supervillain's weapon and superheroes can't give in to their evil powers."

Sawyer looked hesitant on that one but, realizing what he was doing, quickly lifted his little shoulders.

Jenny fought smiling.

"And the third rule is the most important one of all."

Jenny waited with more interest than Sawyer.

"Superheroes must smile lots because smiles boost one's powers and ward off villains."

Sawyer blinked. "Smiles?"

Tristan nodded. "Absolutely. The more you smile, the better superswimmer you're going to be."

"So, if I smile enough, I'll be a better swimmer than Freddie?"

Tristan glanced at the stuffed turtle Jenny held. "I've never seen Freddie that he wasn't smiling, so you've got your work cut out for you on that one, kid."

Sawyer bared his teeth in a smile so big the corners of his mouth squished his cheeks.

Happiness spread through Jenny and she covered her mouth to cover her own smile.

Tristan laughed. "That's a really great start. I think I felt your superpowers growing."

Sawyer's smile morphed into a more real one.

"Let me check to be sure." Tristan reached out and took Sawyer's hands. Jenny's breath caught at the sight of her son's tiny hands in Tristan's strong, capable ones. Hands that had held hers the night before, that had cupped her face while they'd kissed. "Yep," he continued, moving to a shallower area, "your powers are growing. Now, the first thing we are going to do is that, while holding my hands, you're going to come into the water. I've got you, so remember not to let any villains douse you with self-doubt."

Sawyer took a deep breath then slid off the side of the pool and into the water. Tristan held on to his hands. "Great job," he praised, easing Sawyer into the water to stand on his own feet. "That was perfect."

"I'm not scared of the water," Sawyer declared, but stayed close to Tristan. "Mom has brought me to the pool before and I played in the water, but it was only up to my knees."

"That's a great head start on today's lesson. So, this next step is a super easy one and I'm going to do it first." Tristan got on his knees and managed to dunk his head completely under the water.

Water droplets ran down his face, his throat, his muscled chest. Resisting the urge to fan herself, Jenny swallowed.

Brushing his hair back from his face, he grinned at Sawyer. "Now, let me see you do that."

With only a moment's hesitation, Sawyer did exactly as Tristan had done.

Jenny clapped, to which Sawyer bowed.

"Perfect, except your mom didn't clap for me."

"You need affirmation?"

His eyes twinkled. "From you? Absolutely."

"What's af-for-mation?" Sawyer asked, tugging on Tristan's arm.

"A reinforcement and acknowledgment of doing something well."

"Mom, clap for Mr. Tristan, too," Sawyer insisted. "He needs af-for-mation."

"I'll keep that in mind the next time he does something well," Jenny promised.

Tristan's grin had her breath catching and she half expected him to say something flirty. Instead, his focus returned to Sawyer, who was clinging to his every word. "Now, let's walk to the other side of the pool. You want to hold my hand, or you got this?"

As an answer, Sawyer took off for the other side of the pool, Tristan quickly falling into step beside him. Together, they tapped the side of the pool, high-fived each other, then turned to head back toward Jenny.

"Woohoo! Good job, guys! Y'all rock," she said with exaggerated enthusiasm and fist pumps.

"Good job, Mommy."

Lips twisting, Tristan nodded. "Right. Good affirmation, Jenny."

Tristan led Sawyer through a few water games, allowing Sawyer to become more and more relaxed in the water and mesmerizing Jenny with how great he was with her son.

"Okay, next up is your flying lesson."

Sawyer's eyes widened again. "I'm going to learn to fly?"

Tristan tousled his hair. "With a little help. Ready?"

His hand around Sawyer's waist, Sawyer's arms stretched out in front of him as Tristan guided him over the water's surface as if he were flying across it.

"Look, Mom, I'm flying," Sawyer called, his giggles melting Jenny's heart.

"I see that." She also saw the complete adoration in Sawyer's eyes when he glanced up at Tristan.

She wasn't so sure that the same didn't shine in her own eyes.

* * *

"Remember we just got back from camping," Tristan said as he unlocked his apartment door so Jenny could take Sawyer to the bathroom. He'd come in that morning, brought in his gear and unpacked clothes, but most of his equipment sat right where he'd put it next to the front door.

"No worries," Jenny said. "I'm not going to white-glove test the baseboards."

His scrutiny automatically dropped to the baseboards. The clean baseboards, fortunately.

"The bathroom is this way." He pointed them toward the bathroom. "Help yourself."

When Jenny started to follow Sawyer into the room, he frowned. "Mom. I can do it. I'm not a baby."

"Right. I knew that." She smiled at him. "Okay. Don't bother anything."

He gave Tristan that "Moms!" look then went into the bathroom. Tristan wasn't surprised at the resounding click of the lock.

"I… Sometimes I forget how grown up he's getting."

"Nothing wrong with wanting to take care of your kid."

She smiled. "Thank you for that, but I'm positive that, in this case, he wouldn't agree with you. I think I embarrassed him."

"No harm done."

She smiled again then wandered around the open apartment, pausing to look out the window before turning back to him. "You're sure you actually live here?"

He furrowed his brow in question.

"Other than your gear by the front door, this could be anyone's home."

"This isn't a home, Jenny. It's just a place to sleep while I'm in Chattanooga."

"Is there a home somewhere?"

Clammy heat burned his skin. "What do you mean?"

"You've mentioned several places where you've lived during your childhood and as an adult, but is there somewhere you go to be 'at home'?"

"My life isn't like yours, Jenny. There is no building I walk into and get warm fuzzies. To me, houses, apartments, tents—it's all the same. Just a place to sleep."

"And in these places where you just sleep, you never try to make them feel…homey?"

"Why would I do that? I don't plan to stay."

"Do you have any family, Tristan?"

"My father works construction. I'm a lot like him, living in an area until the job is done then moving on."

"And your mother?"

Nausea twisted his stomach. "She passed a few years ago."

Sorrow darkened Jenny's eyes. "I'm sorry."

Tristan was spared having to say that it hadn't mattered by Sawyer's opening the door.

"I'm all done," he announced, rubbing his hands together.

So was Tristan, because he didn't like Jenny making him look around his bare-bones apartment and comparing its emptiness to the warmth of her house.

Not her house, her *home.*

CHAPTER NINE

"YOUR NOSE IS PINK."

Jenny glanced across the hospital bed at Laura. "I got a little too much sun this weekend."

"I didn't notice it this morning before we left the campsite," Laura pointed out as she tucked in a fresh sheet.

"Yeah, about that, what's up with you bailing on me and my having to ride back with Tristan alone?"

Laura smiled. "You should be thanking me for being such a good friend."

"I was thinking of trading you in for a more loyal model," Jenny countered.

Laura and Jenny maneuvered their heavily sedated patient back onto the bed. "Go ahead, if you can find one, but a more loyal friend doesn't exist. I'm the best there is. You're so lucky."

"So you've been telling me since kindergarten."

Laura laughed. "You'd think you'd believe me by now."

Jenny's stare met her friend's, knowing that she did believe her. Not that there had ever been any doubt. Still. "I need you to stop throwing Tristan and me together."

"Because you've realized he's a great guy?"

"He is a great guy." An amazingly great guy who had the body of an Adonis and a heart of gold. "That was never in question. However, I'm not looking for a guy, much less one who will be gone in a few months."

"Don't you think he'd be a good one to cut your teeth on, though?"

"What?" Jenny gasped at her friend's suggestion.

"You know, dip your toes back into the dating scene. The fact that he's only going to be here for a few months is a plus. That way, if you're so rusty that you screw up royally, no big deal. He'll be gone and no one will be the wiser."

"Or I could just not and save myself a lot of hassle."

"But there's no fun in that. Admit it. You had a great time with him this weekend."

She had. Even more so that afternoon with Sawyer. How had Tristan convinced her to eat with him prior to Sawyer and her leaving his place? They'd only been going inside for Sawyer to use the bathroom and dry off, not to stay for grilled cheese sandwiches, which was the only thing he'd offered that Sawyer had said yes to.

"Your entire face got too much sun," Laura teased as they checked to make sure all the patient's lines were still in place. "Pink looks good on you. So, tell me what happened."

"He came back to the house around lunchtime." Making the admission felt liberating, as if confessing that Tristan had been at her house made it a little less taboo. Not that it was taboo. Just…

Laura's jaw dropped. "You invited him over? You sly girl."

Jenny shook her head. "That's not what I said. I left my hat in his 4Runner and he brought it by."

Why was it so much more difficult to tell Laura about Tristan than any of the other secrets she'd shared with her bestie over the years? Even with Geoffrey and Carlos, she'd not held back in telling Laura all the humiliating details.

Laura gave a thumbs-up. "Nice. Women have been using the 'leave something behind' trick for years. I'm proud of you, Jenny!"

"I didn't purposely leave my hat." Had she been a fool to confess so much? Probably, and she wasn't done yet. "He offered to give Sawyer swim lessons."

Laura clasped her hands together. "Oh, Jenny, that's wonderful in so many ways. This shows he isn't like Carlos, and I know how upset you've been that the classes were full. When does he start?"

"Whether or not he's like Carlos is irrelevant. Although, ultimately, he'll leave just as Carlos did. As far as the lessons, today."

"What?" Laura's hands clasped together. "I knew it. Your nose isn't pink from this weekend. You were out in the sun with Tristan. Did you have a great time?"

Yes. She had.

"Sawyer did. I sat poolside while he and Tristan were in the water."

"I don't blame you. That man has a beautiful body, all rippling muscles and brawn."

Jenny rolled her eyes, but Laura continued. "How was it?"

"The water? Cool, but not bad compared to the river."

"Not the water." Laura snorted. "Sawyer and

Tristan meeting. I know what a big deal that is to you."

"He's all Sawyer talked about during our drive home from his lesson and then he had to tell Mom everything, too." She sighed. "He's pretty infatuated."

"And Sawyer's mom? Is she infatuated, too?"

Jenny sucked in a deep breath and shrugged. "She's trying to keep her wits about her, but he doesn't make it easy."

Laura gave a low squeal. "I knew it. From the moment I saw you two together, I knew it."

"We aren't together."

"Not from lack of wanting to be on his part. The man is crazy about you."

Nervous energy zapped through her. "How can you be sure?"

"Have you seen how he looks at you? Jenny, when you're anywhere near, he can't take his eyes off you. And, for the record, you suffer from the same affliction. It's why I don't feel even a smidge of guilt for throwing you together with him."

Jenny didn't deny it. She was certainly suffering from some type of affliction.

"Also, for the record, in all the years I've

known you, I've never seen you so taken with someone. Not even he whose name I won't say because he doesn't deserve to have his name said, or the jerk who came after him."

Jenny wanted to deny what Laura said but couldn't. Seeing Tristan with Sawyer, watching how wonderful he was with her son, had toppled any doubts. She was taken with Tristan.

"I'm not sure what I should do," Jenny admitted, hating how vulnerable her feelings toward Tristan left her.

"How about you quit worrying about what you should do, and just enjoy the next couple of months?"

"That's pretty much what he said Saturday night when—" She gave a tight smile. "I wish it was that easy, that I could just turn off the voices in my head."

"Oh, you mean when you two snuck off from the campfire?" Laura waggled her brows.

"I helped him put burn ointment on where I burned him with that flaming marshmallow," Jenny noted. "Although, I'll admit, I didn't realize you'd even noticed as you seemed quite cozy with Steve. Forget Tristan. Tell me what's up with you and rafting boy."

As they pulled off their PPE, Laura laughed. “Me and ‘rafting boy’ are good. I’m seeing him tomorrow.”

“Tomorrow?”

“He’s busiest on the weekends,” Laura told her as they headed to the nurses’ station.

“I guess that would be the case. Just be careful, Laura. He’s not exactly stick-around-forever material, either.”

Laura’s brow arched. “Because he’s younger than me or because he works for a rafting company?”

“He probably meets lots of women that way.”

Laura snorted. “Sure, he does. That doesn’t mean he drives almost two hours to see them.”

“Probably not, but you seem to be diving in. I don’t want you hurt when he probably goes through a lot of women each summer.”

“You’re wrong,” Laura insisted then shrugged. “But if so, then I’ll count myself lucky that I was one of them. He lives in Georgia but has worked for the rafting company the past three summers. He’ll be starting an internship next summer with a law firm in Atlanta and says he’s enjoying every moment of this last summer of freedom.”

“And you plan to help him do that?”

Laura nodded. "Every chance I get. He's a great guy."

"You just met him."

"Sometimes, you just know these things, you know?"

"No, I don't know."

"Sure you do. You knew it when you met Tristan, but you're too far stuck behind those walls you built after Geoffrey to realize it. Quit hiding and get back to living, Jenny."

"What are you two lovelies talking about?" Roger asked as he and Tristan joined them at the desk. Roger had just had a new admit that they'd gotten settled.

Jenny and Laura exchanged looks then Laura turned toward Roger. "About how you're turning thirty in a couple of months and we're planning to come out to support your big face-plant."

"Let's hope that's not what it is." Roger laughed. "Just a couple of months left in my twenties. That's not that long."

"And yet a lifetime's worth of memories can be made in much less time," Tristan said, his blue gaze meeting Jenny's. They'd been busy since shift change and she'd only caught glimpses of him up to this point. Looking into his eyes, she saw the answers to the questions that had plagued her since arriving. Tristan planned to take her lead on how they acted around each other. The ball was in her court to do with as she pleased.

"Jenny tells me you're giving Sawyer swim lessons," Laura blurted out, forcing the issue. "She also mentioned how great you were with him and how cute you were in your birthday suit. I mean—" she giggled "—your swimsuit."

Jenny guffawed at her friend's claim. "Oh, yeah, I'm trading you in. Y'all have fun. I'm going to chat with Mr. Rossberg."

Later that night Tristan ended up in Mr. Rossberg's room with Jenny. He'd been stable for over twenty-four hours but showed no signs of regaining consciousness despite decreased sedation.

"Tell me more about what you said to Laura about my birthday suit."

"We both know that I didn't say anything about your birthday suit to Laura."

He laughed. "Just wishful thinking on my part then."

Jenny stared at him. "You'd have been happy if I'd discussed you with Laura?"

Helping her to roll Mr. Rossberg so he could be washed, he pointed out, “She's your best friend. If you're discussing anything about me with her, that's a good sign.”

“A good sign of what?”

“That you aren't immune to my charms.”

“We established my lack of immunity on Saturday night.”

Keeping a firm hold on Mr. Rossberg, his lips twitched. “I need a reminder.”

“You won't be getting one.”

“That's disappointing to hear. You know how I need your affirmation.” Her eyes lifted to his and, grinning, he added, “Plus, I've been looking forward to our next kiss.”

Jenny sucked in air. “You're impossible.”

“Where you're concerned, I'm possible,” he assured her. She bit into her lower lip and longing hit him. “As a matter of fact, the only thing that seems impossible is my not kissing you again.”

“Is that why you volunteered to teach Sawyer to swim?”

He shook his head. “I did that because he needs to know how to swim.”

She stared at him a moment, shock registering in her eyes. “You're telling the truth.”

One brow lifted. “Did you think I wasn’t?”

“I thought…well, you know.”

“You thought it was because I want to spend time with you? You’re not wrong, Jenny,” he admitted, wanting to be completely transparent with her. “I do want to spend time with you, but my teaching Sawyer to swim is about Sawyer and keeping him safe. He’s a great little guy.”

Pride brightened her face. “Thank you. He is wonderful. I’ll feel so much better knowing that he can swim.”

“Sure thing. I do have one request, though.”

“What’s that?” she asked, finishing washing Mr. Rossberg then putting a fresh hospital gown on him.

“I want you to get in the water with us.”

“Me?” She paused in straightening the gown. “Wouldn’t my being there just be a distraction?”

“You’re a distraction no matter where you are, Jenny. You distract me.” Night. Day. Swimming. Working. Sleeping. Dreaming. She seemed to never leave his mind.

“I… I’m sorry. Or maybe I’m not, because you’re a distraction to me, too, so it would be unfair for this distraction to be one-sided.”

Pleasure at her admission filled him. Even

more so that she was smiling as she said it. Her walls were still there, but she'd opened the gates, letting him in, at least temporarily.

"You'll bring Sawyer over tomorrow afternoon?"

She nodded. "We'll be there, but I'm making no promises about getting into the pool with you. Just message me when you wake up and I'll bring him by after I pick him up from preschool."

Good. He looked forward to seeing Sawyer. And Jenny. The swim lessons were a win-win as he found giving them gave him great satisfaction, as if he was making a difference in the kid's life during their short time together.

He wouldn't think about that yet, when he'd leave and not be a part of Jenny and her son's lives. Then again, he usually didn't stress about leaving at all.

There was nothing usual about Chattanooga, though.

"You won't be asleep?" he asked, not liking where his thoughts had gone. He wasn't even close to leaving, so he sure shouldn't be stressing about it already.

"I'll go to sleep after I drop him off at preschool in the morning. If you wake up early, then I'll still be asleep."

From across the hospital bed, he eyed her a moment. "How about you message me when you wake up? I'm sure I get more rest than you do, so I don't want to wake you if you're still asleep."

She amazed him with all she managed to do, between work, mother, daughter, and her house.

"My alarm will go off at three."

"That's not a lot of sleep." She really should get more rest.

Jenny shrugged. "It's enough, and spending time with Sawyer before going into work is important. Way more important that getting that extra sleep."

"You're a good mom, Jenny."

Cheeks flushing pink, she gave a nervous laugh then smoothed out the white blanket covering Mr. Rossberg. "You could tell that from meeting Sawyer once?"

"I could tell that from seeing you with him, listening to you talk about him this weekend. I wish I'd…" He stopped, knowing what he'd been about to say but halting that train of thought. "He's a lucky kid to have you for a mom."

"I don't know about lucky, but he's loved."

"That's why he's lucky." Battling memories of his childhood that were trying to surface, Tristan took a deep breath. "You think Mr. Rossberg is enjoying our conversation?"

Jenny smiled. "Normally, when I'm in here, I hope he hears every word, but maybe not so much when I'm with you."

"You hear that, Mr. Rossberg? I think it's time for you to wake up so you can have a real conversation with your nurse."

"I sure hope you wake up soon," Jenny told the man, touching his arm. "Your family would be thrilled, especially your lovely wife. She's ready to take you home just as soon as you're able."

Watching her with her patient, something moved inside Tristan's chest. Physiologically, he supposed that was impossible unless it was a gas bubble, but he'd swear something monumental shifted at the gentleness with which Jenny cared for her patients, her son, even with the way she was with her mother.

Jenny cared for those around her.

When she glanced up and their eyes met, he had to tamp down the urge to wrap his arms around her and hold on for as long as she'd let him.

Yeah, Chattanooga was different, and all because of the woman smiling at him.

Sawyer shook his head, slinging water in a three-hundred-and-sixty-degree direction.

Jenny held up her hands, shielding herself with the fluffy beach towel she held. “You’re like a wet puppy.”

“I want a wet puppy.” Sawyer wiggled as Jenny wrapped him in the towel.

“Puppies are big responsibilities,” she commented, patting him dry.

Wide eyes the same color as her own met hers. “I have responsi-billies.”

Jenny grinned, resisting the urge to hug him to her. “No promises, but I’ll think on it, Sawyer.”

Sawyer turned to where Tristan had joined them. “Do you have a dog?”

Water droplets falling onto his broad shoulders, Tristan shook his head. “I travel a lot.”

Jenny’s eyes were traveling a lot, following the path of those drops as they rolled downward. She visually traced one down his chest and abs until it disappeared at his waistband, then gulped as heat spread through her.

"Couldn't you bring a dog with you when you travel?" Sawyer asked.

Seemingly oblivious to the effect he was having on her internal temperature, Tristan considered Sawyer's question. "I guess I could. I never had a dog while growing up, but I remember wanting one, too. My dad always said it wouldn't be fair to an animal to move around as much as we did, and I took him at his word and have never really given getting one much thought as an adult."

Jenny studied Tristan, noting the way he averted his glance from her as if he didn't want her to see his eyes. He wrapped a towel around his shoulders and made a play at drying off from where he'd been in the pool. Maybe he hadn't been quite as oblivious as she'd thought.

Or maybe his mind was somewhere else completely. That was where hers should be. Somewhere other than how attractive she found his body, because seriously? Was she really looking at his hairy legs and wondering how they'd feel brushing against her smooth ones?

"As long as you love him and take care of him, it would be okay to get a dog, wouldn't it, Mommy?"

Nothing like Sawyer putting her on the spot, but at least his question had her dragging her eyes from Tristan. "It would depend upon your job, Sawyer. Tristan works long hours. What would his puppy do all day while he was at work?"

"Play," Sawyer said as if it were a no-brainer. "When I grow up, I'll have a dog." His face squinched up with thought then brightened. "I'm going to have a dozen dogs!"

"A dozen?" Jenny and Tristan asked simultaneously.

Sawyer nodded.

"What will you do with a dozen dogs?" Jenny asked.

"Love them and play with them," Sawyer replied, dancing around in his towel.

"Good answer, kid," Tristan told him, earning a grin.

Jenny laughed. "Don't encourage him."

"It could be worse."

Jenny arched her brow in question.

"He could be asking for a pet s-n-a-k-e."

Jenny gave an exaggerated flinch. "Nope, not happening."

Sawyer glanced back and forth between them. "What did he spell?"

"Tristan thought you might prefer a reptile to a furry puppy," Jenny explained.

"I want a frog and a puppy," Sawyer clarified then turned to Tristan. "My grammy likes frogs, but Mama says I can't have one to keep in the house."

"Frogs like being outside. It's where their food and friends are."

"But if she'd let me keep one in the house, I'd be his friend and give him food," Sawyer explained, his expression genuine.

"There's that." Mouth curving upward, Tristan glanced toward Jenny. "What say you, Mom?"

"That puppy is looking better and better."

Tristan kept his hands around Sawyer's waist, helping glide the boy over the water as he paddled around, arm floaties in place. His support wasn't needed, but until Sawyer said he could let go, then Tristan would keep his hands on him.

"Look at me, Mama," Sawyer called, splashing around. "I'm swimming."

"You're doing great, Sawyer," Jenny praised from where she sat at the side of the pool. Some days she sat on the edge with her feet dangling in the water and some days she sat beneath a sun umbrella to keep out of the sun. Always, she slathered up her fair skin with sunscreen. Sawyer's, too.

Tristan had offered to help with her sunscreen a few times, but she'd just smile and tell him she had it. She had it, all right. She had him in a jumbled mess of hyperawareness of every move she made.

Even with his focus on Sawyer, his body zoned in on where she sat poolside with her feet dangling in the water.

Both he and Sawyer repeatedly tried to convince her to get in the water with them, but she'd not done so. Had it not been for the rafting trip, he'd have questioned whether she could swim.

"He's a natural." Tristan praised Sawyer's efforts. "I think he may be part fish."

Sawyer giggled. "I am. Swish, swish, swish." He stroked his arms back and forth as Tristan had shown him. Pride filled him. The kid really was picking things up fast.

Jenny laughed. Her face was lighter, brighter, than Tristan had ever seen her.

Jenny loved her son. No wonder. The kid was awesome. Probably because he was Jenny's. He'd not heard Sawyer mention his father, nor had

Jenny, but more and more Tristan grew curious about where the man fit into their lives.

"I'm a hungry fish," Sawyer announced, making chomping sounds as he moved through the water.

"A shark?" Tristan asked, laughing as he launched into some *da-dum, da-dum, da-dum* sound effects.

"Yes!" Sawyer didn't get his reference, just nodded and continued to bite at the water as Tristan "swam" him from one side of the pool over to near where Jenny's feet dangled in the water.

"We'd better feed this fish before he gobbles us up."

Uncertainty settled into Jenny's eyes. "We're taking up so much of your spare time. I don't expect you to go with us to eat. We don't want to be a bother."

"You're no bother," Tristan assured. "I love seeing how quickly our little shark is progressing. Before long, he'll be doing cannonballs off the diving board."

Sawyer splashed his hands in the water. "What's a cannonball?"

Tristan told him, and Sawyer twisted to stare

up at him, floating on the water with Tristan's hand beneath his waist. His floats wouldn't let him sink, but Sawyer wasn't confident enough yet to venture away from Tristan's assistance.

Sawyer's eyes were wide. "Can you do a cannonball?"

"It's been a while, but yeah, I can cannonball."

"Show me," Sawyer requested. "I want to see."

Tristan's gaze met Jenny's and she shrugged.

"Okay, hotshot shark," he told the boy in his arms. "But if I've gotten too old for this, your mom will have to dive in to save me."

Sawyer's expression filled with concern.

"I'm kidding," he quickly assured him then lifted the boy to sit beside Jenny on the pool ledge. "The cannonball is pretty basic. You stay here next to your mom while I jump, okay?"

Sawyer nodded.

"Don't you make me have to come in to save you, Tristan Scott," Jenny warned, pulling her hat brim lower to shade her face.

His challenge met hers. "Would you save me, Jenny?"

"You shouldn't risk it," she warned, a smile playing on her lips. "I might not be strong enough to pull you out."

But he had no doubt that if he were in trouble, she would do her best to save him.

"Guess I won't attempt my double backflip then." He placed his hands to each side of Sawyer. "What your mom is saying is that even when you've been swimming for a long time, it's still always smart to use your brain and not take unnecessary risks. And never swim alone. You shouldn't be afraid of the water, but you should respect it. Always."

Sawyer nodded. "I like swimming with you."

"Ditto, kid. Ditto."

It was true. Tristan did like swimming with Sawyer and was so proud of how the kid no longer seemed afraid of the water. Soon, he'd be all over the pool with just his arm floaties and then Tristan would wean him away from using them.

Tristan swam to the ladder and climbed out of the pool to walk to the diving board. "Watch closely," he called to Sawyer. "Because, before summer is over, I bet you will be doing cannonballs, too."

Tristan stood on the tip of the diving board then bounced into the air, tucked his legs up beneath him and wrapped his arms around them.

"Cannonball," he yelled just before he hit the water, making a big splash.

"Yay!" Sawyer cheered.

He swam over to where he could see Sawyer's and Jenny's submerged feet, then came up right in front of them, slicking his hair back from his face.

"That was great," Sawyer exclaimed.

"You want to do one?"

Sawyer's eyes were wide.

"He can't get on the diving board yet," Jenny noted, sounding a little mother-hennish.

"He doesn't have to get on the diving board. I was going to let him jump in and I'll catch him."

"With him doing a cannonball?" Jenny looked dubious.

"Well, it might be better if he does a shark instead."

"What's that?"

"It's where you put your hands out in front of you then jump."

"Isn't that just a regular dive?"

Tristan shook his head. "Nope. It's the shark. Now, stand up and put your hands up." He demonstrated what he meant.

"Like this?" Sawyer perfectly mimicked Tristan's every move.

"Exactly like that. Now, when you're ready, I want you to jump in to me."

Without hesitation, Sawyer did just that, jumping in.

Despite the boy's floats, Jenny's breath sucked in so hard Tristan heard it over the pounding of his heart in the seconds before his hands closed around Sawyer's waist and he lifted him up through the water and into the air.

"You did great, kid!"

Sawyer shook his head, squinting at Tristan as water ran down his face. "Again!" he cried. "Again. Again. Again."

Tristan laughed.

"You've started something now."

"Who needs the gym when they have a boy in the pool?" Tristan teased. He caught Sawyer a dozen or so more times before Sawyer remembered he was hungry.

Wrapping his little arms around Tristan's neck, he looked him in the eyes. "Since I did good, can we have pizza for lunch?"

"Kid, you did so good you can have filet mignon for lunch if that's what you want."

"Pizza," Sawyer repeated then leaned over and play bit his shoulder. "I'm a hungry shark."

"Sawyer! Tell Tristan you're sorry."

"He was just having fun." Tristan hadn't been prepared for the playful nip. It hadn't hurt but had caught him off guard.

"Biting is not okay," Jenny insisted, frowning at Sawyer.

"But I'm a shark. Sharks bite."

"Well, Mr. Shark, you're in time-out because Tristan isn't shark food."

Sawyer's facial expression fell.

"Really, it's okay, Jenny. He barely nipped me, and it didn't hurt. It didn't even leave a mark." He glanced at his shoulder. "Much," he amended, giving her a wry grin. How did she ever discipline the kid? One tiny pout and he was ready to give him whatever he wanted. "I guess we should have fed this little shark when he first told us he was hungry."

Tristan and Sawyer got out of the pool. Sawyer stayed close to his side, avoiding going to his mother as long as he could. Tristan understood. Jenny had not looked happy about the bite.

But when Sawyer made it next to her, she didn't yell or scream, as Tristan's own parents would have done had he done anything they'd disapproved of. Instead, she looked Sawyer in the eyes and talked to him in a low voice.

Sighing, Sawyer nodded then turned to Tristan. "Sorry I bit you."

"No worries, kid." He hated that the boy had gotten into trouble, but he had to admit that watching Jenny parent Sawyer was fascinating. Not that everything about her didn't fascinate him. It did. From the light freckles that the sun had kissed the tip of her nose with to the love that shone in her eyes for her son.

"Go grab our bag from the table, okay?" she asked him. "Walk, don't run."

Sawyer nodded and took off fast-skipping.

Jenny's attention immediately went to the slight red mark on Tristan's shoulder. "I'm mortified he did that. I can't believe he bit you."

"He's a kid. Kids do silly things. I hate that you had to scold him on my account. You didn't have to."

"I didn't want him to think that was okay. I can't have him biting another student at preschool or when he starts kindergarten this fall."

Made sense, and he felt a little less guilty. "You're a good mom, Jenny."

She gave him an odd look. "Because I don't want my kid biting other kids? I'd say that's pretty basic parenting."

She might be surprised at how little basic parenting some moms and dads did. How little his own had done. He'd generally been an afterthought.

"I meant in how you handle him altogether," he clarified.

"Most of the time it's more of a figure-it-out-as-I-go kind of thing." She gave a nervous laugh. "I worry that I'm going to do something that messes him up, you know? That as an adult he'll be in therapy and they'll tell him it's all my fault for being a terrible mom."

"If he has to go to therapy, it won't be because you're a terrible mom, Jenny. You're a great mom."

Her cheeks pinked. "Thank you."

"He's doing really well."

"I couldn't believe he jumped in like that. It's a little scary, honestly."

"He's got this. I'm going to work with him tomorrow without his floaties."

"You think he's ready?"

He nodded. "I know he is. Like his mom, he's a natural."

"You've not seen me in the water to know whether I'm a natural or not," she reminded him.

"About that..." he teased, waggling his brows as he moved toward her.

"You wouldn't." But as she said it, she started scooting away from him.

Laughing, Tristan scooped her up. Her body was warm from the sun and his was growing hotter by the second from having her in his arms. Skin against skin, to where every fiber of his being was aware of hers.

"Put me down, Tristan," she insisted. Even as she wrapped her arms around his neck, she squirmed to get free. "I should remind you that the last person you held bit your shoulder."

He mentally groaned as an image of Jenny love nipping his shoulder hit.

"You're not going to do the same, are you?" And, if she didn't quit squirming, he was going to embarrass them both.

Her gaze locking with his, her arms still around his neck, she stilled except for where her fingers had threaded into the hair at his nape.

"You know I'm not. Just as you're not going to throw me in the pool."

Goose bumps covered his body at her fingers entwined in his hair. He wanted her. From the moment he'd met her, he'd wanted Jenny. "You think not?"

"You don't have a death wish, do you?"

He laughed. "You don't scare me, Jenny."

Although, truth be told, the way her fingers toying at his nape had his body responding as if he were a puppet on a string, the way she felt in his arms, the way he felt looking into her eyes, the way he felt when he was with her and Sawyer, terrified him.

So much so that without another thought, Tristan shifted his weight and dropped into the pool with his arms still holding Jenny close.

Maybe the dunk would do something to cool off his libido and ease his crazy thoughts.

"I can't believe you did that," she sputtered as she came up from the water, clinging tightly to him.

Holding her close, as he wasn't sure how strong her swimming skills were, Tristan stared down into her beautiful face, her beautiful wet face. "Oops. I must have lost my footing."

Jenny scoffed. "Right. That's exactly what happened."

"I knew eventually you'd come into the water to play," he teased, thinking the cold water hadn't eased his reaction to her in the slightest. If anything, her wet body wrapped around his only served to heighten his awareness.

"I should have known it would be because you tossed me in," she accused.

"I never let go of you, Jenny, nor will I." Realizing what he'd said and how powerfully those words shook him to his very being, he cleared his throat and added, "In the water, I mean."

CHAPTER TEN

WHY HAD TRISTAN'S voice broken? Jenny wondered, clinging to him.

Had he felt he needed to clarify what he'd meant?

They both knew he would let her go. When his time in Chattanooga was up, he'd leave, and she and Sawyer would be left behind.

The thought of him gone broke her heart because it was difficult to imagine returning to life without him. Her son was crazy about him. She was…she was pressed against him, their bodies wet, his arms holding her waist, her arms around his neck, and their faces were so close that his breath teased her lips.

If she wanted to kiss him, all she had to do was lean in just a little and their mouths would touch.

"Jenny," Tristan said, his voice almost a growl. Hunger filled his eyes. He must have realized how mere centimeters separated their mouths, how her wet body was wrapped around his as they bobbed in the pool water.

Her gaze dropped to his mouth. She knew how talented that mouth was, how precious his lips, and how his kisses made her crave things she'd thought forever gone.

"Kiss me," she whispered, needing to feel more than his breath on her lips.

"Now?" Tristan's voice held surprise. Surprise Jenny understood because he'd put her under a spell that she couldn't seem to break. "Yes. Now. Later. Tonight. Kiss me."

Tristan's breath sucked in. "You drive me crazy, you know that?"

"No more so than you drive me," she countered, staring into his eyes and cupping his handsome face. "I want you to kiss me."

"Jenny," he moaned, leaning his head toward hers.

"Hey!" Sawyer shouted from the side of the pool, holding their swim bag. "I didn't know you were getting in the pool."

"Neither did I," Jenny called, her gaze not leaving Tristan's. His whole body had tensed at Sawyer's interruption. Or maybe that had been hers. She couldn't believe she'd forgotten Sawyer was there, that she'd become so entranced with the gorgeous man holding her that she'd abandoned herself to his charms.

"I convinced your mom to go for a swim," he said, looking toward Sawyer.

With his attention on Sawyer, Jenny seized her moment. With all her might, she jumped upward then came down with as much force as she could, pulling Tristan under the water with her. When they came up, she wiggled to free herself and made a beeline out of the pool.

"Run, Mama. He's after you!" Sawyer warned, jumping up and down at the edge of the pool and giggling with glee.

Jenny was swimming as fast as she could, but she was no match for Tristan.

"Argh!" she squealed as his hand clasped around her, turning her to him.

"You know I have to make you pay for that, right?"

"You started it," she returned, her chest heaving from her escape efforts.

"Did I?" His eyes sparkled more brilliantly than sunshine bouncing off water. "Make no mistake, Jenny, we've barely begun."

"He caught you, Mama!"

Tristan had caught her. In more ways than one.

His time in Chattanooga was rapidly ticking away. He could say they were barely started, but their time together was already over half gone, and making the most of every precious second left seemed more and more imperative.

"You're going to love the jellyfish," Sawyer told Tristan as he gave them a personal tour through the Tennessee Aquarium as if he was on their payroll. "And in the next section there's penguins."

"Penguins?" Tristan looked impressed. "Real ones?"

Sawyer nodded. "When I grow up, I want to work here and take care of the fish and birds who live here."

"That sounds like an interesting job," Tristan admitted, his look meeting Jenny's as he gave her hand a quick squeeze. Jenny couldn't help but smile and squeeze back.

Look at her, acting like a giddy teen, holding hands and making googly eyes, she thought. No wonder. Every moment away from work was spent with Tristan one way or another. Swimming lessons, eating, taking Sawyer to the park, and even during household chores, he was by her side. Deep down, she knew she was making his leaving that much worse by letting him consume her every moment. She also knew that she wasn't strong enough to push him away. Soon enough, he'd be gone.

Until then she'd…she'd what? She didn't know exactly how to label what was happening between them, but whatever it was put joy deep in her belly, and Sawyer's, too.

"Mama likes penguins, too," Sawyer continued, pulling against where he held Tristan's other hand, "but she likes people best because she wants to take care of them. I want to take care of animals."

"You prefer the two-legged kind of animals, eh?" Tristan asked, his eyes twinkling as he winked at Jenny.

"The two-legs kind?" Sawyer asked, his face contorting with lack of understanding.

"He means people," Jenny clarified for her son. "And, yes, I do. I can at least see them coming." She gave an exaggerated shiver. "Snakes don't have legs."

Tristan grinned then shared a look with Sawyer. "Maybe we'll see more snakes before we finish our tour."

Sawyer nodded. "We will. Big ones and little ones."

A commotion up ahead caught Jenny's attention. A seventyish woman lay on the floor and a gray-haired man knelt beside her.

"Bess?" He shook the woman, but she didn't respond.

Jenny glanced toward Tristan, but he was already rushing that way. To his credit, he hadn't let go of Sawyer's hand, and her son was skipping along beside him to keep up.

Jenny took off after them.

"Sawyer, stay right here," Tristan ordered as he knelt next to the couple. "Hi. My name is Tristan. I'm a nurse, and this is Jenny. She's a nurse, too. What's going on and can we help?"

"We were walking around, looking at the fish, and my wife collapsed to the floor," the man told him, relief showing on his face at their appearance. "Please help."

"Have you called 9-1-1?" Jenny asked. The man shook his head and Jenny pulled out her phone to make the call.

"Is it okay if I check her?" Tristan asked as

he leaned in to see if the woman was breathing. "Soft, but steady breaths. Pulse is regular but bradycardic."

"What does that mean?" the man asked, fear in his voice. "Is she going to be okay?"

"Her heart rate is a little slower than normal," Tristan explained, lifting the woman's feet. "Here, I want you to hold her legs up like this. Sawyer, you okay, bud?"

"Huh?" the man asked, but did as Tristan said.

Sawyer nodded. "I can hold a foot."

"Just stay close because we may need you to help do that," Jenny said, proud of how calm he was and for his offering to help. Still on the line with the emergency operator who'd just promised to dispatch an ambulance, Jenny turned back to the man, "Does your wife have any health problems?"

Clasping the woman's feet, the man nodded. "Not recently. She had a heart attack last year but has been doing good. Her cardiologist cleared her to go on this trip. She's diabetic and—"

"She's diabetic? What was her blood sugar this morning? Do you have her meter with you?" Tristan asked from where he had his ear pressed close to the woman's chest, attempting to listen to her heart sounds.

"I'm not sure if she checked it this morning. We woke up late and were running behind. She does have a meter. It's in the car, I think. We're parked in a lot nearby. Do you want me to get it?"

They were in the middle of the aquarium. Jenny hoped they had the woman revived or further assistance there long before the man would have time to go to his car and get back to them.

A growing crowd had gathered around them and Jenny asked, "Does anyone have a glucometer? How about a glucose tablet or something sweet? Maybe a piece of candy?"

Someone produced a meter kit and handed it to Jenny. Another woman gave a chocolate bar.

"Can someone get us a soda or juice in case her sugar has dropped and we need it?" Jenny asked as she knelt next to Tristan. "I'll prop up her upper half if you want to try giving her some of this."

He nodded, broke off a small piece of the chocolate bar and placed it in the woman's mouth. Once it was there, he unzipped the glucometer kit, turned the machine on, cleaned one of the woman's fingertips with alcohol then popped her with a lancet. It wasn't ideal since he didn't have gloves, but he carefully got a drop of blood into the test strip.

Within seconds, the machine's display read thirty-eight.

"She has hypoglycemia, meaning her sugar is too low. That's why she's unconscious. We need to get her sugar up." He checked the woman's mouth then placed another tiny piece of chocolate beneath her tongue. "Does anyone have anything else sweet? A packet of sugar, even?"

Jenny supposed it was possible someone might have such an oddity in their purse, but no one spoke up.

"Sir, you can gently put her feet down. Tristan had you holding them up in case she wasn't getting good circulation to her heart, but that doesn't seem to be the problem."

Fortunately, the guy who'd taken off to find a pop machine was back with a bottled soda and handed it to Tristan.

"Let's get some of this in her, stat," Tristan said, twisting off the cap.

Phone cradled between her ear and her shoulder as the dispatcher continued to talk, Jenny held the still-unconscious woman's head up to where Tristan could carefully pour some of the soda into her mouth.

Sweat drenched the woman's skin and dampened her hair. Jenny knelt to use her thighs to leverage the woman so holding her in an elevated position was easier.

Sawyer moved next to Jenny, putting his hand on her shoulder. "Is she going to be okay, Mommy?"

Hating that he was witnessing the hypoglycemic event, but so proud of how brave he was being, Jenny nodded. "I think so, honey. Her body doesn't use sugar properly and hers is too low, so her body is trying to protect her by letting her sleep until we can get her sugar up. Once we do that, she should wake up and she'll start feeling better."

His little hand patted her. "I hope so."

Jenny hoped so, too.

"Bess?" the woman's husband said, bending over her. "Can you hear me, Bess? Your sugar is low, but these people are helping you. Wake up, Bess."

"What's your name, sir?" Jenny asked, hoping to get him to move from over the woman's face.

"Felix."

"Felix, can I get you to step back a little?" Tristan asked. "It would be great if you would hold Bess's hand and keep talking to her so that when she wakes up she isn't as frightened. Tell her she's okay."

The man did as Tristan asked.

Tristan kept putting small amounts of soda in the woman's mouth, making sure she reflexively swallowed before adding more.

Soon, Bess's eyes popped open and she began to come around.

"Mama! She's awake," Sawyer exclaimed, jumping up and down. "It worked!"

"Ma'am, I'm Tristan and this is Jenny. We're nurses. Your blood glucose dropped too low, and you lost consciousness. We've been working to get sugar in you. Can you take a drink for us?"

Staring blankly at him at first, her eyes shifted to her husband then back to Tristan. "You're doctors?"

"Nurses," Tristan repeated, checking the woman's pulse, again.

"Okay," the woman said, scooting as if to sit up.

"Take it slow," Jenny encouraged, helping her

into a sitting position and continuing to support her in case she got light-headed or passed out again. "We don't want you going out on us."

"Drink, Bess. It'll make you feel better," Felix urged, giving his wife's hand a squeeze. "You sure scared me."

By the time the ambulance arrived and the paramedics got to them, Bess was sitting up and sipping on the soda. She was still pale and clammy, but should be fine once the aftereffects of her hypoglycemic episode wore off.

"Thank you for your help," Felix told them, shaking their hands.

"No problem," Jenny replied, hoping that it really wasn't, and that Sawyer wouldn't be bothered by what he'd witnessed. She glanced around, looking for where her son had gone and didn't initially spot him.

Hunkered by an octopus display, he watched them.

Going over to him, Jenny squatted next to him. "Hey, big guy. You sure were brave."

"I didn't feel very brave."

Jenny wanted to wrap him in a big hug. "Are you kidding me? Those superhero lessons have been paying off. You were amazing."

His expression brightened. "Do you think Tristan thinks so?"

Because Tristan was his superhero. No wonder, with the way he doted on her son. Watching him interact with Sawyer the past few weeks had her doing a bit of hero worship, too. He wavered from responsible adult role model to playful kid at heart. With her, he was steadfast, smiling, attentive, willing to keep things on the lowdown at the hospital, not that she didn't think her coworkers knew something had changed since the rafting trip. Everything had changed and yet, really, nothing had. When the time came, Tristan would leave, and she doubted she would ever be quite the same.

"I'm sure Tristan thinks you were brave. How could he not when you were such a great help?" She gave Sawyer that hug as much for herself as him, kissed the top of his head, then straightened. "Now, how about we go find those horseshoe crabs you were telling me that we could touch?"

After Jenny closed Sawyer's bedroom door, Tristan followed her back into the living room. Her mom must have gone to bed while they were in Sawyer's room because Geneva was no longer watching television.

Rather than sit or ask him to sit, Jenny hesitated just inside the vacated room, nervously fiddling with her shirt hem. "Thanks for helping me get him to bed. He loved that you sat with him while I read his stories."

"It was my pleasure. He's a great kid," Tristan told Jenny and meant it. He'd never spent much time around kids, but Sawyer was the best. And when he smiled, Tristan's insides did a funny flip-flop because of the genuineness. "I was so proud of him today at the aquarium. I've seen grown adults not handle situations as well as he did."

Leaning against the back of the sofa, Jenny smiled. "I was proud of him, too. I was worried that it might have bothered him more than he let on, but he seemed okay, didn't he?"

Tristan nodded. "After dinner, he heard me call Felix to check on Bess and heard me say she was doing great, that they checked her out in the emergency room, decided it was truly just a hypoglycemic episode, and they discharged her. Other than telling his grammy how his mommy was a hero, he's not mentioned it. I think he'll be fine."

"Ha. It wasn't me he kept referring to as a hero. It was his favorite swim instructor."

Tristan smiled. "His only swim instructor."

"There is that. Thank you for teaching him, for taking us to the aquarium, and for burgers and ice cream afterward. And for…well, everything. He adores you."

Her words warmed his insides. "I promised I'd take him if he swam from one side of the pool to the other, and he did."

"While wearing his arm floats."

"That counts. Besides, he'll be able to do it without his floats soon enough, too. For now, it's important he knows I keep my promises."

Jenny's gaze lifted and Tristan's stomach clenched at the emotions swirling in those honey depths. What was she thinking? Because, if he didn't know better, he'd think she was wondering if he planned to keep his promises to her. The only promise he recalled making was that he wouldn't hurt her, at least not intentionally.

He'd do his best to keep that promise. The last thing he wanted was to cause Jenny pain. He wanted her to smile when she thought of him.

"We're still on for swim lessons in the morning?"

She nodded. "As long as you don't mind. I worry that we're taking up so much of your free time. You've mentioned all the things you'd planned to do while living in Chattanooga and instead you've spent most of your time with us."

"Plans change." For the better, because no hike or tourist attraction could possibly have been as fulfilling as spending time with Jenny and Sawyer. He regarded her for long moments as she picked at a loose string along her shirt hem. "Are you ready for me to leave?"

She hesitated. "Do you want to stay for a while, Tristan? We could watch a movie or play a game or something."

"What kind of game?" he asked, curious and wondering if they weren't already playing a game that could be dangerous to both their emotional well-being.

"Most of what we have are kids' games."

"Candyland and Hungry, Hungry Hippos?"

Her lips twitched. "We have those."

"I imagine Sawyer would be upset if he discovered we'd been playing those without him."

"You're right. He would," she conceded then

glanced around her living room as if searching for something to entertain him with. Didn't she know he'd be content to just sit and hold her hand? "You want to see what's on television then?"

He wasn't ready to leave, so he nodded. "Is there anything in particular you want to watch?"

"I'm not sure what's on. I don't watch much television, so whatever you want to watch is fine."

Tristan sat on the sofa, but rather than pick up the remote, he turned to Jenny and stared at her.

"What?" she asked, her cheeks pinkening in the soft glow of the lamplight.

"You told me I could watch whatever I wanted."

She eyed him curiously. "And you're looking at me?"

"There's nothing else I'd rather be looking at."

The soft glow of the lamp illuminated her flushed cheeks. "You're so smooth with the words."

Was that what she thought? That he was feeding her lines?

"I'm stating the obvious."

"That you want to look at me?" she asked,

tucking her hands beneath her thighs as she continued to lean into the sofa.

"Surely you know that by now? I can't not look at you whenever you're near. Not touching you at work is a lesson in discipline and patience, but I agree with you that it's best for you that we carry on as close to as we were before as possible."

"I don't want people feeling sorry for me after you leave. I think they're going to, anyway, but the less they know, the better." Her glance cut toward the hallway leading to her son's bedroom. "I… Would you want to sit outside? Sometimes I sit in the porch swing at night and just think."

"About?" he asked, following her to her back patio.

Outside, a warm breeze carried the sweet smell of the honeysuckle vine growing along her fence.

Picking up a pillow, Jenny took a seat on the two-person swing. "Lately? You're what I think about."

CHAPTER ELEVEN

HIS CHEST EXPANDING at her admission, Tristan sat next to her and laced his hand with hers. "I'll take that as a compliment."

Twisting toward him, she tucked one leg beneath her. Rather than look at him, she stared at their interlocked fingers, visible in the light filtering out from the house. "You should. I never dreamed I'd let another man get close to me again."

Her raw admission had him lifting her hand to his lips and pressing a kiss there. "I'm glad you did, Jenny. The past few weeks have been wonderful."

Rather than verbally answer, she squeezed his hand.

"Sawyer's dad hurt you?"

Her flinch revealed as much as her words. "He did, but only because I let him. I should have known better."

How any man could have had Jenny and Sawyer and let them go was beyond Tristan. The man had been an idiot.

"Tell me about him."

Sighing, she straightened and gave the swing a little push so they began to sway back and forth, the creak of the chains creating a soothing rhythm. "Geoffrey was a gorgeous, successful doctor, and I was a naïve nursing student doing a clinical rotation at the hospital where he worked." She paused and he wondered if she'd said all she was going to say, but then she continued. "He was older than me. Eighteen years older, but at the time, thirty-eight to my twenty didn't seem like a big deal. All that mattered was that he showered me with attention, and I fell head over heels for him without remembering that if something seemed too good to be real, it was."

"He was married?" Tristan guessed.

"Close. Engaged."

"Engaged yet dating you?"

She nodded. "He was wonderful, sending flowers and doing lots of little things that made me feel special." She made a humph sound. "I thought he loved me, and we'd be together forever, so I quit saying no. After that, our relationship was just about sex on his part, right up until I got pregnant. He wanted me to get an abortion."

Pain shot across Tristan's chest at the thought of Sawyer having never existed. "You obviously didn't do that."

"No. My mom was a single mom. She could have chosen not to have me but didn't. Instead, she raised me with love, and I had a great childhood. I never considered doing anything other than the same when I realized I was pregnant."

"Does this doctor help you with Sawyer?"

Jenny sighed. "He paid child support until I finished nursing school. After that, I offered to let him sign over all rights to me in exchange for a small lump sum to be put into a college fund for Sawyer. He jumped at it and never batted an eyelash at signing away all his parental rights." She pulled her hand free and rubbed her palms over her bare arms. "He just kept saying he couldn't believe how little I asked for when he'd have paid more to be rid of me and my 'brat.'"

Her voice wobbled and so did Tristan's emotions. "He's a fool."

"I think so, but his loss is my gain. Prior to that, I'd worried that he'd show up for his visitation and eventually might want to take Sawyer from me." She glanced his way and met his contemplation with sad eyes. "I guess that sounds really bad. I wouldn't have kept Sawyer from his father, but when I knew he didn't want him, didn't love him, it would have been devastating to watch him drive away with our baby."

Tristan couldn't imagine the agony of having that happen. "I'm glad you never had to."

"Me, too, mostly. Having seen Sawyer with you this summer made me realize that he needs more male influences in his life, though."

"Not his father, surely?"

She took a deep breath then exhaled slowly. "I wouldn't stop Geoffrey from seeing Sawyer if he wanted to, but I don't think he ever will. He and Sonya are married and have two kids now."

"Poor woman."

Jenny shrugged. "She knew what she was getting and didn't care. She knew about me, confronted me to let me know I wasn't the first and wouldn't be the last, that she knew Geoffrey was a beautiful man and that women found him attractive. I… I was shocked at how little she was fazed that he'd been cheating on her for months and that I was pregnant. I'd have been devastated." A strangled noise sounded from deep in her throat. "I was devastated."

Her pain ricocheted through him and he pulled Jenny to him, wrapping his arm around her to hold her close. "Of course, you were. Any sane person would have been. Sounds as if they deserved each other."

"I guess so. I haven't talked to them in years, not since he gave Sawyer to me. With them living in Ringgold and him being a physician, I hear his name from time to time, but that's it."

"I'm surprised you continued to live here."

"This is my home, Sawyer's home, and where I want to raise him. My mother is here. I have no plans to ever leave Chattanooga, especially not because of a man."

Tristan had no plans to stay.

"You're sneaky—you know that?" Not that Jenny minded Tristan surprising her with a day trip to Atlanta.

"Some would call it romantic," he pointed out, grinning at her as he held out his hand to help her down from the 4Runner.

Taking his hand, Jenny stepped onto the concrete floor of the crowded parking garage. "Is that why Sawyer's not with us?"

Guilt played across his face. "I considered bringing him, but your mom suggested that he stay with her."

Jenny sighed. "She's matchmaking."

"That doesn't bother me."

"It should, because she's planning on you sticking around awhile." Forever was more like it. With the slightest encouragement, her mother would be booking a wedding venue.

More guilt flashed. "We both know I won't, Jenny."

"It's not me you have to remind," she quipped. "I'm well aware that this time next month, you'll be gone."

He started to say something, but Jenny held up her hand. "Let's not have this conversation today." Or ever. "It's been a long time since someone has surprised me with something 'romantic' and I just want to enjoy the day without overanalyzing."

Hesitating a moment, he nodded. "Then let's hope your team wins."

"They will," Jenny assured him, waiting as he

opened the back hatch. “What’s that?” she asked when he handed a bag to her.

“Another surprise.”

Feeling a little giddy, Jenny looked into the plastic and laughed when she saw its contents.

“I didn’t know how else to have you dressed for the part without giving away what we were doing.”

Pulling the jersey out of the bag, she realized there were two.

“One’s for me. I figured you’d suspect if I had it on when I picked you up this morning.” He took the larger shirt from her then pulled his T-shirt over his head.

Hello, biceps and abs. Had the temperature just gone up several degrees or what? She slid her fingers into her pockets in an effort to keep them from exploring the indention that ran down his chest and disappeared into his shorts. The man had a beautiful body.

“If you pull out a giant foam Brave’s finger, I’m going to think I died and went to heaven,” she said to distract herself from the view.

“If a foam finger makes you happy, we can buy one on our way into the stadium.” He gestured at the jersey she held. “Your turn.”

Jenny laughed. "Yeah, right. Nice try, but I'm not changing in the parking lot."

"Have it your way," he teased, tossing the shirt he'd removed into the back and picking up a clear heavy-duty plastic bag that contained hats and sunscreen. He clasped her hand. "Come on. You can change into your shirt while I'm grabbing some drinks and dogs."

"Oh, baby, this really is a romantic surprise."

"You'd rather have candlelight and caviar?"

"No way." She wrinkled her nose and began singing "Take Me Out to the Ball Game."

"Yes!" Jenny yelled, jumping up from her seat as the Braves' third baseman caught a pop fly, finishing the inning.

"Having fun?" Tristan asked, grinning at the jig she was dancing and wondering at how even her goofy movements stirred his insides in ways no woman had.

"Are we winning?" she countered.

He gestured to the scoreboard. "We are. Seven to four."

"Which is why I'm smiling and having fun."

He laughed. "You wouldn't be if we were losing?"

Glancing at him, she gave him a big, teeth-showing smile. "Does that answer your question?"

He laughed again. "You're welcome."

Settling back into her stadium seat, she lifted her gaze to his. "I really do appreciate you bringing me today."

"I know. I was teasing you."

"I just didn't want you to think I was ungrateful."

"I didn't. I've seen the pure joy on your face as you've bopped around with excitement."

"It's an exciting game." The fans began chanting and she joined in. "Mom brought me a couple of times when I was younger, but this is the first time I've been to a game since Carlos and I—"

"Who's Carlos?"

She wrinkled her nose at him. "Seriously? You want to discuss my ex-boyfriend today? You don't see me plying you for all the nitty-gritty details of your past relationships."

"No, I don't want to discuss an ex-boyfriend today." *Or ever.* "And, there's not much to tell you about my past relationships."

Her eyes narrowed. "Don't try to convince me

there are no girlfriends past, because I won't believe you."

"There are girlfriends past, but none that really mattered."

"Because you've never stayed in one place long enough to fall for someone?"

"Apparently falling for someone doesn't require staying in one place for very long."

Realizing what he meant, she gave him a cheesy smile. "Are you saying you've fallen for me, Tristan Scott?"

"You know I have."

"You are a sweet-talker."

He knew she was trying to make light of what he was saying, but making sure she knew she was special felt imperative. Maybe because he knew her past relationships hadn't gone well.

"There's never been anyone like you, Jenny. You're a fantastic person. Smart, funny, an amazing mom and a great kisser."

"Speaking of kissing—look!" she gestured toward the stadium. Glancing that way, he saw they were up on the JumboTron. "I think we're supposed to kiss now."

Tristan didn't need to be told twice. Leaning toward her, he grinned then pressed his mouth to hers for a kiss. Probably because they were being watched, she made a wide-eyed, gob-smacked, happy expression when they pulled apart.

"Did I mention that you're a great kisser?" he asked, reaching for her hand.

Eyes shining brightly, her lips curved. "The way you're looking at me makes me believe that."

The way she was looking at him made him want to believe in a lot of things. That was pure craziness.

"The truth must be on my face, then," he told her, leaning in and stealing another quick kiss.

"Thank you, Tristan," she whispered when they parted. "For everything. I've had a great time."

"The day's not over yet." Excitement filled him at what else he had in store.

She arched a brow at him. "There's more after the game?"

He nodded and she glanced down at her shorts and Braves' jersey. "Whatever it is, I hope it's casual."

The Braves won their game, but Jenny was convinced she was the real winner. How had

Tristan pulled off passes to meet some of the team? She'd gotten a ball autographed by two of her favorite players and another she didn't know much about as he was a rookie but was sure she'd grow to love.

"Just wait until Roger and Laura hear about what we did today," she mused from the passenger seat as they traveled north up I-75. "They're going to be so jealous."

"You plan to tell them you spent the day with me?"

Although he was looking at the road, Jenny rolled her eyes. "You think Laura doesn't grill me at the beginning of every shift, wanting to know if I saw you and, if so, what happened and how did that make me feel and what did you say and blah, blah, blah?"

Tristan took a quick side look. "What do you tell her?"

"That you are giving Sawyer swim lessons and…" She paused, trying to decode her emotional ramblings to her best friend. She liked him, but she was going to get hurt. He was a phenomenal kisser, but that was as far as they'd gone physically. Her pulse launched into orbit when he was near, but her brain kept saying to proceed with caution.

"And?" he prompted when she remained silent.

"And I like you." There, she'd admitted what all her ramblings were about. She liked him. Jenny liked Tristan. A lot.

"What does Laura say to that?"

"That she's happy for me and that I should throw caution to the wind and have as much fun as I can for as long as I can."

"Sounds like Laura."

Jenny nodded. "I'm sure Roger knows, but he doesn't say much, just smiles and occasionally gives a nod of approval when he catches me watching you." Heat flooded her face. "I, um, not that I watch you a lot, but…well, you know."

"Watch all you want, Jenny. I'm flattered you'd want to look my way." Appearing thoughtful, he tapped his fingers against the steering wheel. "There's probably no way for our coworkers not to know when they see us together."

"You think we're that obvious?"

"That I want you is stamped over every fiber of my being. I imagine they see that, that you see that, when our eyes meet."

Jenny's breath sucked in. Yeah, she saw, but

hearing him say the words aloud added depth to the intense sexual chemistry that was always present no matter how much she questioned or tried to squash it.

"You think they assume we're having sex?"

He shook his head. "I'd guess the opposite. There's a certain familiarity that comes with having sex."

Trying to decipher what he meant, she asked, "You mean that we wouldn't want each other as much?"

"I didn't say that," he quickly corrected. "That first kiss proved that everything we share is just going to make me want you that much more. I'm talking about the way a couple touch and look at each other when they intimately know every nuance of the other."

Jenny's heart pounded. Her eyes closed. What would it be like to know every nuance of Tristan's body? Of his lovemaking?

He'd never pushed for more than a kiss, probably because she'd claimed abstinence and he was respecting that. She liked that he honored her wishes and didn't push the issue, only...well, more and more she longed to turn her dreams into reality.

* * *

"Do you have to go?"

Tristan's heart broke at the sadness in Sawyer's eyes. Eyes that were so like Jenny's. He'd seen that sadness there the past few days as their time together dwindled. Saying goodbye to Sawyer was almost as difficult as saying goodbye to Jenny was going to be. He'd never wanted kids, couldn't imagine possibly putting a child through what his parents had put him through, and yet Sawyer made him think he was missing out on something wonderful.

When he left Chattanooga, he *was* going to be missing out on something wonderful. The boy in front of him and his mother.

But that didn't mean he could, or should, stay.

"I do have to leave, bud. My job is finished."

From where he sat at Jenny's kitchen table, Sawyer asked, "Couldn't you find a new job?"

Tristan's heart ached. "I already have a new job. In Chicago."

Sawyer sighed. "Is that far away?"

"Pretty far." Too far. Forever far.

Sawyer glanced over to where Jenny leaned against the kitchen counter. "Will your car drive there, Mama?"

She flinched, her face pale, telling Tristan everything he needed to know about her thoughts on his leaving. She didn't want him to go, either. Maybe he could arrange his schedule so he could fly to Chattanooga once a month to see them. It wouldn't be nearly enough, but at least it would be something.

Jenny knelt beside her son. "Sawyer, Tristan will be busy when he moves. Even if I could get off work, he isn't going to have time for us to visit. He'll be working and having to unpack his stuff and having new adventures."

Jenny's explanation had Tristan pausing. He'd been about to offer to fly them to him or to fly back to Tennessee. Despite her earlier reaction to Sawyer's question, there was something in her voice that warned him he should remain silent and let her explain this to Sawyer.

As far as new adventures, life beyond this room loomed unenticing.

"We could help him," Sawyer insisted. "He likes my help."

"I have work, he has work, and you'll be starting kindergarten soon," Jenny said with resignation. "Grammy would miss us."

"Grammy could go, too." The kid had a comeback for everything Jenny said. "She likes Tristan. She says he's good for our family."

Jenny sent Tristan a pleading look. One that said *Don't make me the bad guy here.*

He took a deep breath then looked Sawyer directly in the eyes. "I'm going to miss you, too, kid, but I have to go, and you have to stay here. That's the way life works sometimes."

"I don't want you to go." Sawyer's lower lip trembled, and Tristan would have sworn the floor shook. He felt that off kilter, that jolted.

"I know, Sawyer. You make me not want to go."

That was the truth. He'd never had trouble leaving a job. Leaving was what he did. What he'd always done. His whole life. It's what his dad had done. What his mom had done. It was all Tristan had ever done. All he'd ever known and thought he wanted. Yet…

"Maybe I can come back to visit someday."

Aware that Jenny was frowning at him, Tristan hugged Sawyer, breathing in the scent of kids' shampoo, savoring the feel of Sawyer's tiny arms wrapped tightly around his neck.

"I hope so," Sawyer told him, hugging a little tighter. "I don't want you to forget me."

"Never going to happen," he promised, kissing the top of Sawyer's head. The affection had been instinctive, impulsive. "I'll always remember you and how proud I was of you for jumping off that diving board and swimming to me. You're unforgettable, Sawyer. Never doubt that."

Yeah, he'd not wanted this, but Sawyer and Jenny made him wish he did, because imagining not having them in his life boggled his mind.

Or was that his heart?

Jenny wasn't sure how much more she could take of the lovefest going on. She was having a hard enough time at the thought of Tristan leaving, of how her insides were shattering, of how she didn't know how she was going to go back to the contentment she'd known before him when she'd experienced such happiness with him. But hearing the pain in Sawyer's voice, seeing how distraught he was, was pure torture, riddling her with guilt that overshadowed her own pain.

She'd known better than to let Tristan into their lives. She'd known he was leaving, had known that letting her son get close to him would only lead to heartache. She hadn't known how hungry Sawyer was for a man in his life, hadn't been prepared for Sawyer to latch onto Tristan and fall so in love with having a male influence.

"That's right. That dive was unforgettable. Superhero worthy." She gulped back the tears forming in her eyes, willed herself to be strong, and pasted a smile to her face. "I was proud and nervous for you."

Sawyer tossed Tristan a "Moms!" look.

"I never doubted you, but I'll admit I was nervous, too," Tristan said, ruffling Sawyer's hair. "You did great. Keep practicing and you might make it to the Olympics someday."

"What's the Olympics?"

Jenny rested against the kitchen counter, watching while Tristan explained what the Olympics were in a way a four-year-old could understand.

The rest of the evening, Sawyer stayed close to Tristan, taking the quickest bath in history, and insisting that Tristan help tuck him into bed.

"Will you read my bedtime story?" Sawyer's wide eyes pleaded with Tristan. Jenny reminded herself not to be hurt, that Tristan would be gone the following day, and this was Sawyer's way of holding on until the last second to the man who'd become such an integral part of their family.

"I… Okay. If that's what you want. You pick one."

Sawyer went to his bookshelf, glanced over his options, then pulled out two books. He glanced her way. "I thought you would want to read one, too, Mama."

Smiling, Jenny nodded. "You know I do."

"I see what you did there, kid," Tristan said, laughing low. "Smart move, getting two bedtime stories."

Feigning innocence, Sawyer held up his books. "Which one do you want to read?"

Tristan glanced at the books then chose the one with a big red dog on the cover. Climbing into his bed, Sawyer scooted over and patted his mattress.

"You have to sit beside me when you read, that way I can see the pictures."

Tristan nodded and complied.

When Jenny continued to stand, Sawyer frowned. "Mama, you can't see the pictures."

She was too busy staring at Tristan and Sawyer cuddled together reading the story to look at the book anyway. Never would she have imagined how much the image choked her up, made her knees weak, her head spin.

That, she thought. *That's what I want.*

What she couldn't have.

"I'm fine," she managed to say despite her tight throat.

But Sawyer wasn't having it and Jenny sat on the opposite side of him. Not that it helped her to see the pictures. Her eyes blurred with tears.

Still, she held herself together, laughed at the appropriate times, and relished the warm little body next to hers who was her whole world and whom she wanted to protect from every ache and pain the world might throw his way.

Sawyer giggled. He asked questions. He looked up at Tristan with pure adoration and hero-worship, and Jenny found herself doing the same. Why couldn't he have wanted to stay in Chattanooga? Why did he have to leave when she and Sawyer cared so deeply for him? When they didn't want him to go?

When it was her turn, Jenny took the second book and focused on the words.

"Mama, you're not reading it right," Sawyer insisted, frowning. "You didn't make the caterpillar be me."

Jenny tended to edit stories to feature Sawyer as she read them to him, making him the main character of each adventure, making things happen to him, and he loved it. She'd just been reading the words without any animation or Sawyer ad-libs. No wonder he was speaking up.

Telling herself to get her act together, she threw herself into the story, making it as animated as she could, pausing to have her fingers form a mouth to munch on his belly a few times. Sawyer giggled, turned to Tristan several times to make sure he was paying attention, and looked at him with complete adoration.

"One more?" Sawyer asked when she finished, yawning even as he did so.

Jenny shook her head. "You've had a big day and it's already quite a bit past your bedtime."

"But I'm not tired." Another yawn escaped.

"Good night, Sawyer." She kissed his forehead. "I love you to the moon and back."

"And across the oceans and all the lands," he said, completing their ritual.

Jenny's heart squeezed.

"Night, buddy." Tristan touched his arm. "Sleep tight."

Sawyer's eyelids appeared heavy, but he wasn't so tired as to have forgotten what was happening. "You'll be gone when I wake up?"

Tristan nodded.

A mixture of a yawn and a sigh escaped from Sawyer. "You can stay here if you change your mind because we love you."

A strangled sound roared in Jenny's ears. She wasn't quite sure if it had originated from her or Tristan, just that she could barely breathe at her son's innocent declaration.

No, they did not love Tristan.

They didn't.

Sawyer might, but she didn't.

She wanted him to stay, but she didn't love him. She couldn't.

Only, whether she wanted him to be or not, Sawyer was right.

She loved Tristan.

CHAPTER TWELVE

"HE DOESN'T MAKE leaving easy, does he?" Tristan asked when he and Jenny went to the living room. Sawyer had been sound asleep almost before they'd closed his bedroom door.

"He's never had anyone he's felt close to that's left, so it's hard for him to comprehend that you're going to be gone."

Tristan sat on the sofa, ran his fingers through his hair. "His childhood is so different from mine."

Jenny sank onto the opposite side, tucked her leg beneath her, and turned toward him. "In what ways?"

"All I knew was leaving," he admitted, surprised at how much he was about to tell Jenny when he'd never talked to anyone about his childhood, and yet he didn't hold back. Telling her made what he would be doing the following day easier. Knowing would help her understand why he couldn't stay.

"After my parents split, I was back and forth between them, but I mostly stayed with my dad. He worked construction and was constantly on the move, rarely waiting for a job to finish before moving to another. Changing schools two or three times during a year was nothing."

"Goodness," Jenny breathed.

"Mom stayed in the South, but only lived in a spot long enough to run up bills she couldn't and wouldn't pay prior to taking off," he continued, not liking the pity in Jenny's eyes, but knowing he was unable to stop the train wreck he'd started. "I was shuffled back and forth between them just enough to give the other a break to mess up their lives a little bit more."

"That must have been hard on you."

He hadn't liked it. The going back and forth, the never having anything more than he could carry with him because he never knew what, if anything, of his things would still be there when he returned. Or where he'd be returning to. It had been much better to never get attached to things or people because they were interchangeable in his parents' world. Nothing had been sacred.

"It's all I ever knew, so I'm not sure I'd say it was hard." He'd just accepted it as the way things were, never questioning the constant moves too much to begin with. It had been all he'd known. He couldn't recall exactly the point that he'd realized his way of life was so different from his classmates'. Maybe it hadn't mattered because by that point leaving was as much a part of who he was as it was his parents'. He expected to leave, had formed every friendship with the knowledge that it would eventually end. "It was just different from Sawyer's."

Jenny nodded. "And mine. I've lived here, in this same house, most of my life, and have barely left the state." Her glance met his. "I can't fathom the life you lived as a child."

"It wasn't all bad."

"It must not have been, or you'd have settled down in one place rather than continuing to move around as an adult now that you have control over your fate."

"I doubt I'll ever 'settle down in one place', Jenny." How was that for honesty? "The need to be on the move is in my genes."

"But you could stay if you wanted to," she suggested, her voice barely audible.

Why did guilt prick him? And had that been accusation in her tone?

"You've known from the beginning I wouldn't stay," he reminded.

She nodded as if she understood. He wanted her to understand. But it was obvious she didn't.

"Do you ever miss any of the places you've lived? Or the people you've met?"

"I'm going to miss you and Sawyer, Jenny. What I told Sawyer was the truth. I won't forget him." He met her big honey-colored eyes. "Or you, if that's what you're wondering."

Her eyes shone, biting him with more guilt before she glanced down at her hands. "Yes, I guess I was wondering that. Sawyer sure is going to miss you. He's grown so attached to you."

Sawyer. Yet, in her eyes, he saw the truth. Jenny would miss him, too. How could she not? They'd spent every spare moment together the past few weeks.

"The feeling is mutual." Regarding Jenny and her son. "I've never spent much time around kids, but he's great." The thought of not seeing Sawyer again; of not knowing if he'd continue practicing his swimming… If he'd get that puppy he wanted so badly… If he'd grow up to be a marine biologist or if he'd change his mind on what he wanted to be a dozen times before reaching adulthood… If his hair would stay a pale blond or if it would darken as he aged… If— "I really am going to miss him. And you."

Jenny's throat worked. "I want to say something, feel as if I'm supposed to say something, yet I don't know what to say."

Her voice broke. He could see how much she struggled to appear as if all of this was no big deal, as if his leaving was no big deal. It never had been in the past.

Leaving Chattanooga was a huge deal.

"You don't have to say anything, Jenny." Maybe it was better if they didn't say anything. "Will you move over here and let me hold you one last time before I go?"

She hesitated and he sensed her defenses were already popping into place. He even understood. He didn't want to hurt her and knew she felt pain that he was leaving, knew Sawyer hurt that he was going. But he couldn't stay. He never stayed. He had obligations elsewhere.

If he wanted to stay, he'd eventually leave. It was in his blood. And then what? He'd hurt them even more. Better that he left now than to give a false sense that he'd stick around.

But as Jenny snuggled against him, he wondered what she'd say if he was the type of person who could stay by her side forever. Because as he wrapped his arms around her, he really wished he was that type of man.

"Thank you," he whispered, kissing the top of her head. "I want to put this moment to memory."

Jenny wiped at her eyes.

He nuzzled his face into the softness of her loose hair. "Don't cry, Jenny. Not over me."

He wasn't worth her tears.

"Who says I am?"

Sweat popped out on his skin as her words hit then logic erased his own self-doubts. Of course, she was. Her brave defiance had him smiling despite the ache that he was hurting her.

"Guess that was my own wishful thinking getting in the way of rational thought," he mused, wondering what she'd say if he admitted how much having met her meant to him, wondering what she'd say if he admitted it would be easy to give in to his own sorrow. "Since it's not me causing your eyes to leak, tell me what is."

She sniffed then said, "I realized I'm going to have to find someone else to help me with my yardwork."

Tristan laughed. But just as quickly as the humor hit, it faded. Jenny would find someone to replace him, not just to do yardwork with her, but to spend time with her and Sawyer. She'd smile at someone else, laugh with someone else, hold hands with someone else. Kiss someone else.

The thought gutted him, but the thought of her and Sawyer being alone forever gutted him even more.

"Promise me that you'll let someone help you after I'm gone."

She pulled back enough to stare into his eyes. "I was joking about the yardwork, Tristan. I've always done my own and never expected you to help with that. You insisted, remember? I never asked you to do that."

"I know you didn't expect me to, and I never felt as if you did. I wanted to help you, Jenny. I wanted to make your life easier and to see the joy in your eyes when your projects came together. You need someone in your life." Someone who wasn't him. "I don't want you shutting yourself off from the opposite sex again. Date, enjoy life."

Her gaze narrowed. "How can you sit there and tell me to date and enjoy life after…after…" She took a deep breath. "You and I are different, Tristan. I can't just randomly bring men in and out of Sawyer's life. You were different." She sucked in a deep breath. "You are different."

Tristan's pulse pounded so hard he could barely breathe.

"I didn't want to do this, if you remember. I didn't want to get involved with you because you scared me from the beginning. I… I could barely think straight when you were near. Not just because you're gorgeous, but because there's something about you that I'm instinctually drawn to in ways I can't put into words.

"Even now, I can't look at you and not want to touch you." Her eyes dropped to his lips. "Not want to kiss you." Her gaze lifted. "I can't believe that after tonight, I'll never see you again, Tristan. That I'll never kiss you again." She placed her hands against his cheeks. "Or touch you. How am I supposed to just forget you and 'date someone else and enjoy life' when you're who I want?"

Jenny wanted him. His chest soared at her admission, but warning bells went off just as loudly.

"I'm flattered, Jenny, but you'll forget me."

How many promises had he heard over the

years that someone would never forget him? He'd moved around enough to know that people forgot, they moved on. Jenny would, too.

She shook her head. "You're wrong. That's not who I am."

Tristan gulped back the lump in his throat. "What are you saying, Jenny?"

"Stay with me," she whispered, her hands trembling against where they cupped his face.

That he'd stay forever tempted the tip of his tongue. Sweat drops popped out on his forehead. He needed to leave before he made promises he couldn't keep.

"Tomorrow we'll say goodbye, but give me now, Tristan," she urged, "to abate the rest of my lonely nights. Give me you."

Jenny couldn't believe she was saying the things she was saying.

Panic darkened Tristan's eyes and had heat pouring off his body. Fine. There was panic in her, too. Panic that tonight was the last time he'd be hers and what a fool she'd been not to embrace every moment, every experience, with him to the fullest.

As vulnerable as she felt, she wouldn't back

down. Why should she? Either way, he'd be gone tomorrow.

"You don't know what you're saying, Jenny."

She snorted. "Seriously? I'm a grown woman. I know exactly what I'm saying, and so do you. I'd ask if don't you want me, but I know you do."

Along with that panic, it was in his eyes. She'd seen desire in his eyes many times over the past few months. Tristan wanted her. He looked at her and saw an attractive woman. When he could have had his choice of women, she was whom he had chosen to spend his time with even though she'd refused to have sex with him.

That knowledge emboldened her, fed her desire. Taking his hand into hers, she stood and pulled him to his feet.

His fingers laced with hers. "What are you doing, Jenny?"

But rather than say anything, she led him to her bedroom. When they were inside, she shut the door and locked it, just in case. If Sawyer awakened, she didn't want him coming to her room and surprising them.

She walked over and flipped on her bedside lamp, turned and looked to where Tristan stood by the door. He didn't move, didn't smile, just stared at her as if he was frozen in place. Maybe he was.

Maybe she was dreaming. It felt surreal, as if she floated to him and reached around him to turn off the overhead light. Eyes locked with his, she grabbed the hem of her shirt and pulled it over her head.

Eyes locked, almost as if he were afraid to let himself look at what she'd uncovered, Tristan sucked in air. "Jenny!"

"Shh…" she breathed, putting her finger over his lips. "You have a beautiful mouth, Tristan. I want to feel it against me."

"We can't do this, Jenny. Not now. Not when I'm leaving tomorrow." But even as he said it, he kissed her fingertip. Once. Twice.

"If not now, then never," she whispered, tracing her finger over his bottom lip. "Never doesn't work for me, Tristan. Kiss me."

"Never doesn't work for me, either." Still, he hesitated, cupping her face. "Are you sure, Jenny? This won't change that I'm leaving tomorrow. I don't want to hurt you further."

"I'm sure." To prove it, she slid her hands beneath his T-shirt and lifted it over his head, revealing his broad shoulders and muscled abs.

"Mmm… I've wanted to do this for so long," she admitted, brushing her fingers over his stomach, reveling in how her touch had him sucking in a deep breath.

"As I've watched you with Sawyer in the pool, do you have any idea how unbelievably much I've wanted to touch you here?" She bent and kissed his chest, his muscles tight beneath her lips. "And here." She pressed another kiss to his tight stomach. "And here and here and here."

Goose bumps stood at attention over his skin, and he groaned. "If you don't stop that, tonight is going to be a very quick, disappointing experience for you."

She shook her head. "You're not going to disappoint me, Tristan."

He put his hands around her waist, lifted her to where she looked directly into his eyes.

"You're right. I'm not going to disappoint you, Jenny. Not tonight," he promised. "Tonight, I'm going to give you more pleasure than you've ever known and then I'm going to give you more."

Leaning forward, Jenny pressed her mouth to his, kissing him with all the passion surging through her, kissing him without holding anything back on how she felt. She wanted him.

She loved him.

Tomorrow, he'd be gone, and she'd deal with that then. For now, he was hers and she planned to seize every moment.

Streaks of light began eating away the darkness. It was past time for Tristan to have left. He should have gone hours ago. Instead, he'd lain in Jenny's bed with her warm body snuggled against his.

She'd been asleep since minutes after the last time they'd made love. But other than a quick power nap that had ended when she'd shifted in her sleep, he'd slept very little. The feel of her naked body moving against his had awakened him, and ultimately her, as he'd had to have her again and had roused her with his mouth until she was as hungry for him as he'd been for her.

That had been a couple of hours ago.

He'd ordered himself to leave, but he'd kept delaying, soaking up the feel of her cradled in his arms and unable to bring himself to get out of her bed.

But he was running out of time. To stay longer was to risk Sawyer waking and finding them. Having to explain why he'd stayed the night would be bad enough, but having to say another goodbye to the child, to Jenny, he wasn't sure he could do it.

Carefully, he disentangled his body from hers.

Jenny sighed in her sleep but didn't waken.

Dressed, he hesitated by the door. Leaving had never been this hard, but that didn't stop him from doing so.

CHAPTER THIRTEEN

"HE WAS JUST gone when you woke up?"

Keeping a close eye on where Sawyer ran around the park playground with several other kids, Jenny nodded at Laura's question. Leaning back against the wrought-iron bench they sat on, she sighed. "Maybe it was better that way. For him to just go without tearful goodbyes."

But if that was true, then why did she ache so unbelievably much? When the sunlight streaming in through her bedroom window had warmed her face, causing her eyes to open, she'd felt such happiness until she'd seen the empty spot next to her and known he was gone. That he'd snuck away without telling her goodbye had hit her hard.

"I can't believe he just left like that."

"He and Sawyer had already said their goodbyes." Memories of the night before rushed through her mind, and she swallowed. "I guess we'd said ours, too, just without words."

She'd made love with Tristan. She refused to call it anything else, because what they'd done, what they'd shared, had been so much more than sex.

Glancing at Laura, she gave a tight smile. "I shouldn't be telling you this."

"Hello. Best friend." Laura tapped her chest. "You're supposed to tell me everything."

Jenny nodded. "There is that. Thank you for always being there for me through thick and thin."

"Girl, you do the same for me when I need you."

"Maybe, but it sure seems like I'm always the one who makes a mess of her life."

"Is that how you feel, Jenny? Because when I look at you, I see someone who has her stuff together."

"What do you mean?"

Laura gestured toward where Sawyer was playing. "Look at him. You are doing such a great job raising him."

"Ha. It doesn't feel that way."

"Well, you are. He is happy, and healthy, and has a mama who loves him with all her heart."

"He is a great kid." Echoes of Tristan having

said the same thing the night before rang through her mind. How long would everything remind her of something he'd done or said?

"You not only made it through nursing school, but you did so with honors."

"I don't know if I could have done it without you, especially after I got pregnant. You were a lifesaver."

"You could have, and you would have. It's who you are," Laura assured her. "Our whole lives, you've always known what you wanted. You work hard and never halfway do things. Most of the time you achieve the goals you set out for yourself, Jenny, including buying your mom's house. I've always been so proud of you, my friend."

Jenny sniffed. "No fair making me cry. I've already done that too much today."

"Don't cry. Be happy. You had an amazing three months with one of the hottest guys we've ever met."

"He's so much more than just hot. He's smart, funny, patient, kind—"

"You're in love with him, aren't you?" Laura interrupted.

Jenny took a deep breath. "It would be better if I wasn't."

"Girl, you weren't supposed to fall in love with him, not when you knew he wouldn't stay."

Jenny shrugged. "Like you said, I never do things halfway."

Sawyer came running over to her, his small hands going palms down against her thighs. "Mama, are you crying because Tristan is gone?"

Jenny's heart squeezed that Sawyer immediately thought her tears were due to Tristan. She didn't want him to worry about her or to make his own sorrow worse, so she shook her head. "No, baby. Aunt Laura told me something sad, but I'm just fine."

She would be, too. Laura was right. When Jenny set her mind to something, she could achieve anything. Maybe she took the long, hard route to getting there, but eventually she did arrive.

She'd get there on getting over Tristan to where eventually he would be a fond memory of the man who'd shown her what love could be.

Two weeks had gone by since he had left Tennessee. Two long and lonely weeks.

He missed Jenny. He missed Sawyer. And he was barely into his three-month contract in Chicago. Prior to his Tennessee stint, he'd have enjoyed the breeze off Lake Michigan cooling him as he pounded the pavement during his run. Prior to Tennessee, he'd have taken up the pretty waitress's offer to come watch the theater show she was part of in her wannabe-a-big-star-someday efforts. Prior to Tennessee, he wouldn't have had to exhaust himself to the verge of collapsing just to grab a few hours' sleep. He'd not had problems sleeping since he was a kid.

Now, when he closed his eyes, all he saw was Jenny. Her smile. Her eyes. Her hands as they'd clasped his, tightening and releasing over and over. Her body beneath his. Her soft cries of pleasure haunted his dreams.

Had either of his parents ever struggled to leave someone? Some place? If they had, they'd never let on. He wasn't sure they'd struggled to leave him when they'd dropped him off to whichever one he hadn't just been living with. To the contrary, they'd felt relieved to be free of their parenting burden.

Jenny had struggled with his leaving. Sawyer had struggled. They'd wanted him to stay. Had anyone ever wanted him to stick around the way they had?

Had anyone ever wanted to stick around the way he had wanted to?

Yet, he'd left. Why? Why hadn't he been able to let himself consider staying in Chattanooga to see what happened between him Jenny? Why hadn't he told her all the emotions that had overwhelmed him when she'd come apart in his arms? That he'd never before known what they'd shared in or outside the bedroom?

Pausing to lean forward, hands on his knees, Tristan gasped for air.

He couldn't do this. Not a moment longer.

Before he could remind himself of all the reasons he shouldn't, he pulled out his phone and dialed her number. She didn't answer. Not surprising. It was midday. If she'd worked the night before, she'd be sleeping. Knowing she'd know it was him who had called anyway since she'd have a missed call from his number, he waited to leave a message, trying to think of what to say in the few seconds before the beep prompted him to speak.

How could he convey how crazy he felt without her? How much he missed her and Sawyer?

That he ached to be back in Tennessee? That when he looked around his new apartment all he saw was emptiness?

"Jenny, it's me. I was checking to see how you and Sawyer are doing. Chicago is great. The hospital admin cares about their patients. Not like there, you know, but they're better than most." He hesitated then added, "You should come up here and I can show you around. Then again, I guess Sawyer has started school and you can't. Or maybe your mom can watch him for a few days, and you could come up. Sorry. I'm probably not making sense." Not even to himself. "But I was jogging, and I thought I'd see how you were doing and let you know I was good."

Before he went into a complete idiotic babble, he hung up the phone.

Not his smoothest call, but Jenny had a way of knowing what he was saying even when the right words didn't come out. She'd know he'd called because he missed her.

She'd know he was an idiot for leaving her and Sawyer.

He knew he was an idiot for leaving.

Wasn't that why he'd lain in bed watching her sleep for so long before he'd gotten out and driven back to his rental? He'd not bothered trying to sleep anymore but had packed the remainder of his meager possessions into his 4Runner and headed north. Once, while sitting in heavy traffic on I-24, he'd considered going back, but he wasn't someone who stuck around. Much better to have left the way he had to where, hopefully, her thoughts of him were good.

If she thought of him at all.

She'd said she would, that he had her heart. If that were true, if she really had given herself to him, would it have changed anything?

She had given herself, he scolded himself. She'd never have given her body if he hadn't had her heart.

He really was an idiot.

Jenny clasped her phone long after it had quit ringing. Oh, how her heart had leapt at the number on the screen. And, oh, how she'd struggled not to answer it and beg him to come back to Chattanooga.

Perhaps the thought that she might do just that had been what had given her the strength not to answer.

"Who was on the phone, honey?"

Jenny tucked her phone back into her pocket. "No one, Mom. Now, are you sure you don't want to take more of the dishes with you?"

Her mother shook her head. "Giles already has a houseful. I shouldn't take anything you and Sawyer might need."

"Sawyer and I are just fine. Sawyer is already talking about moving into your room and us turning his old room into a play area."

Jenny's mom gave a watery smile. "This is a lot more difficult that I thought it would be. I should just stay here."

"Mom, you're getting married. Of course you're going to go live with Giles."

"But you might need me. Sawyer might need me. Giles and I can wait on getting married."

"Oh, no. There is no way I'd let you put off your wedding because of Sawyer and me. Giles makes you happy, happier than I've ever seen you. Mom, I can't imagine not having had you here with me during Sawyer's first few years, but the reality is that I'd have been okay, you know?"

Her mother smiled. "I know, but that doesn't mean I have to leave now."

"Actually, it does," Jenny corrected. At her

mother's wide-eyed shock, she clarified. "Not that you can't come back if Giles isn't good to you, but Mom, I know he's going to be great. He wants to love you and take care of you. Sawyer and I will always be here, but you need to go and do you."

Her mother swept her up into a big hug.

"Knock, knock," Giles said, coming into the living room then, seeing them hugged up, stopped. "Am I interrupting? I can come back later if I need to."

"No," Jenny answered, giving her mother one last squeeze. "You're not. You're a part of this family, too, about to be, anyway, and are always welcome."

Giles smiled and wrapped them both in a bear hug. "Same goes for you and Sawyer at our place, right?"

Still teary-eyed, Jenny's mom nodded.

Sawyer poked his head out of his room and frowned. "Y'all are all mushy."

"Get over here so you can be mushy, too," Jenny told him, laughing.

He hesitated then, giggling, ran over to them and wrapped his arms around her and his grammy's legs.

Yeah, maybe life wasn't what it could have been had things been different with Tristan, but life was good.

She'd keep making it better. For Sawyer and for herself.

That would be a lot easier if she cut the strings completely where Tristan was concerned. Taking his calls, even going to see him or allowing him to visit, would only keep the scab ripped off a deeply wounded heart.

A deeply wounded heart that her son had also experienced but seemed to be doing a little better with. He'd only mentioned Tristan twice today so far, compared to the dozens per day he averaged.

As much as she missed Tristan, they'd said their goodbyes.

For the rest of the day she told herself that, even did a decent job convincing herself. But late that night, knowing she was right to keep her break from Tristan clean didn't keep the tears at bay.

Children were much more resilient than broken-hearted women.

"I'm so glad you agreed to go with us to celebrate Roger's birthday."

"Once I mentioned it to Sawyer, he's spoken of little else," Jenny told her friend as she opened the back door to help Sawyer out of his car seat. She'd driven separately from her friends as they'd had to be there much earlier to be ready for their jump. That Roger had recruited several of their friends to make the plunge with him didn't surprise Jenny. If she'd not had Sawyer to think of, she might have done so, too.

"I mean who doesn't want to hang out at a private airstrip and watch your crazy friends jump out of a plane, right?"

Sawyer grinned as he jumped down from the car to the hot pavement. "I wish I was big enough."

Jenny's breaths quickened. "Yeah, well, I'm glad you're not as I'm not quite ready for you to jump out of planes."

Sawyer grinned. "Someday I will be big, though."

"I know," Jenny told him, ruffling his hair. "You're going to be a wonderful young man and I'll be a very proud mother. I am a proud mother."

He beamed up at her.

"And Sawyer could be a proud son as there's still time if you want to jump," Laura teased.

"Not happening. Sawyer and I are here for the show, not to fling ourselves out of a perfectly good plane, but you have fun with that."

Sawyer tugged on her arm. "Mama, can I stand by the fence and watch the plane?"

Jenny glanced over at the metal fence separating the parking area from the airstrip. There were a couple of picnic style tables close by.

"Sure. Go ahead. I'll be there in just a bit." She'd packed a cooler bag with drinks and snacks for while they waited. Plus, she wanted to have sunscreen handy to reapply to herself and Sawyer.

She grabbed her bag from the back, but as the trunk lid was closing, her gaze caught Laura's. The hair on her arms prickled.

"What is it?"

"I need to tell you something. Maybe I should have told you before, but to be fair I only knew for sure last night and I didn't want you to miss out on today if he wasn't really going to be here."

Jenny's breath gushed out of her as surely as if she had dropped from a plane and was plummeting in a free fall.

"If who wasn't really going to be here?" Not that she didn't know. No doubt he was here to jump with Roger as part of the birthday celebration.

"Tristan!"

Jenny closed her eyes, took a deep breath, then glanced to where her son excitedly bounced at the fence, calling to a group that had come out of the hanger.

"Tristan! Tristan," Sawyer called, waving his arms back and forth.

"Someone is glad to see him," Laura pointed out and then gave Jenny a hug. "I've got to go. Forgive me for not telling you, okay? It was for your own good."

Jenny watched her friend jog across the parking area and disappear inside the hanger, then glanced back to where Tristan had come through the fence gate and knelt next to Sawyer.

"I've missed you, too," she heard Tristan telling him as she walked up. Why did each step seem in slow motion? Why did her heart beat so crazily hard? He'd left her without saying goodbye. She could argue that he'd been saying goodbye the entire night, but she couldn't cut him any slack. Not if she wanted to get through the day. She had to hold strong.

"Mama, Tristan is back and is jumping out of the plane, too," Sawyer told her the moment he realized she was close.

"I'm only back for the weekend, bud," Tristan clarified, straightening to his full height prior to meeting Jenny's stare. "I fly back to Chicago on Monday."

Those blue eyes probed hers, left her weak-kneed, left her wanting to throw her arms around him as Sawyer had done. Instead, she kept her cool and gave him a tight smile. "You came in for Roger's birthday?"

Studying her, he nodded. "I'd promised I would do this with him."

"With you living in another state, he'd have understood if you hadn't," she pointed out.

"I wouldn't have understood. I keep my promises."

Her gaze dropped to his lips, saw them moving as he spoke, but in her mind all she could think was that the last time she'd seen him had been in her bed. With that thought came a whole influx of memories better not recalled.

"Tristan, they're ready for us," Steve called from where the group still stood.

He nodded then turned back to Jenny. "I'm glad you two are here. I wasn't sure if you would be."

"We didn't know you'd be here," she said tightly.

"But we're glad you are here, aren't we, Mama?" Sawyer piped up, reminding Jenny that everything they said, did, was being observed by her son, and likely their friends, as well.

"The more, the merrier," Jenny said for lack of knowing how else to answer.

Jenny wasn't happy he was there. Tristan ran his fingers through his hair and sighed. What had he expected? That she'd throw her arms around him in an embrace the way Sawyer had?

He'd known better.

She'd not answered any of his texts or calls since he'd left, including the one he'd made from Roger's the night before.

"I'll see you when I'm back on the ground."

"Wave at me from the sky," Sawyer requested.

"Sure thing." He glanced toward Jenny. "Do you want me to wave at you?"

She hesitated then shook her head. "I'm good, but thanks."

She was good. The best.

Nodding his understanding, he fist-bumped Sawyer and then turned, planning to join his group.

He'd only taken a few steps when Jenny stopped him, her hand grasping his arm.

"Be careful," she said, her voice strained.

His glance met hers. So much swirled in those big eyes of hers that he felt as if he were already free-falling.

"I always am." Except when it had come to protecting himself from becoming too entangled with Chattanooga. Throwing caution to the wind, he leaned forward and pressed his lips to her cheek.

Her eyes not wavering from his, Jenny sucked in a breath.

"We'll talk later," he promised, "after I'm back on the ground. For now, wish me luck."

"I wish you luck."

He took a few steps then turned. She was still standing in the same spot. Her finger was pressed to her cheek where he'd kissed her.

Crazy joy filled him. Crazy because seeing her

filled him with such happiness, but how could she ever forgive him for all the mistakes he'd made and was sure to continue to make? How could a woman as wonderful as Jenny ever love a man whose feet never stayed in one place long enough to make roots when hers ran so deep?

Just beyond her, Sawyer waved with the exuberance the kid showed for most things in life. Tristan waved back and entered the open hanger to join the others who were already being strapped up.

"She's missed you," Laura said from where she stood on the mat, her arms outstretched and her tandem jumper adjusting her straps.

"Maybe," he admitted, shaking hands with the man he'd met earlier and whom he'd be jumping with. "Tell me what to do."

Soon their group was taxing down the runway with lots of whoops and hollers for the cameramen who were recording their jumps.

Jenny, Sawyer and a few others were sitting by the fence, watching as they took off. Sawyer was still waving, and Jenny did the same as the plane rolled past them.

Why did the conversation he planned to have

with Jenny knot his stomach so much more than the fact he was about to jump out of a plane at fourteen thousand feet?

CHAPTER FOURTEEN

JENNY READ SAWYER his bedtime story then tucked him in. Between watching the skydivers and then eating lunch at the mountaintop restaurant overlooking the Sequatchie Valley, he'd had such a big day that he'd not made it to the end of the book before he'd been sound asleep.

She paused in his bedroom doorway a few moments, watching him, then turned off the light and closed his door.

Restless, she cleaned the kitchen, straightened the living room, started a load of clothes, brushed her teeth, then stared at herself in the mirror.

Why was she hesitating to take off her mascara and cover-up? Why instead had she freshened her light application of makeup?

Tristan hadn't said he'd come to see her. All he'd done was say they'd talk later. He could have meant the following day. He may have meant via phone after he was back in Chicago. He may have just been caught up in the moment.

No, he'd been telling the truth when he'd said he kept his promises. He lived by his own honor code and honesty ranked high.

Still, when her phone dinged at just after nine, her breath caught.

I'm in your driveway. Can I come in?

Yes, she typed back, wondering exactly what she was agreeing to. Was he there to talk or for a repeat of their last night together? If the latter, did she have the strength to send him away?

Obviously not, as she barely had her living room door closed behind him prior to his mouth covering hers.

Covering was such a mild word. Devouring. His mouth devoured hers.

When they pulled apart, Jenny's chest heaved with the need for air and her head spun.

"I've missed you."

"I—I missed you, too." It wasn't as if she were revealing some great secret with her admission. No doubt he knew, or he wouldn't be there. "But I just want to talk, not…not…well, you know."

"Have sex with me?"

She nodded. "I don't think we should do that again."

They shouldn't have done it to begin with and yet how could she regret what had been the most pleasurable night of her life? Too bad that pleasure had been followed by such anguish.

"As contradictory as it may seem for me to say, following what just happened, I'm not here to have sex with you, Jenny."

"That's good." Kind of. Another part of her immediately wondered if he no longer wanted her. Surely, he did. His kiss had been as hungry as her own.

"Is it really, my sweet Jenny?" He paced across the living room to stare at a photo of her and Sawyer. "I'm not so sure it wouldn't be easier to show you the things inside of me rather than try to put them into words."

"Why are you here, Tristan?"

"You knew I'd come."

"Yes." She had. "But nothing has changed since you left Chattanooga."

"Everything has changed since I left. At least, in my world, it has."

"I imagine Chicago is very different from my hometown."

"I'm not referring to where I lay my head at night." He snorted. "Or maybe that's exactly what I'm referring to. There's a nurse position that I've been looking at. It's here. I want to come back to Chattanooga, Jenny."

Her heart pounded so loudly its aftershocks could likely be felt miles away.

"I want to come back to you," he continued. "Before I sign the contract, I need to know if that's what you want?"

Fingertips digging into his clammy palms, Tristan waited for Jenny to say something. His declaration seemed to have shocked her, but she must have guessed how he felt?

"You're a grown man. You don't need my permission to move back to Chattanooga."

He ran his fingers through his hair as he searched for the right words.

"I'm not seeking your permission." Although, maybe he was. Maybe he wanted her to say all the right things to make this conversation easier. And maybe that wasn't fair to her. "Can we go sit on the patio?"

He'd been thinking about what he wanted to say to her for weeks, so why he'd stalled for a few extra minutes made no sense. But what about the things he did made sense these days?

He followed her out to her backyard. In the moonlight, he watched her sit in her porch swing and tuck her leg up beneath her.

Knowing he was too restless to sit, he paced across the stones.

"This should be easy. It's not as if I didn't know I'd be in Chattanooga this weekend, that I'd see you, and yet finding the right words seems impossible." He swallowed. "Roger offered me an out to my promise to jump with him, but I refused it."

"Why?"

"Because I hoped you'd be there."

"You aren't the only one who keeps their promises," she declared, lifting her chin.

"I played over how it would be to see you again in my mind what seems like a thousand times."

"Were you disappointed by the reality?"

"My eyes seeing you is never a disappointment, Jenny, but in my mind I'd imagined you running to me the way Sawyer did."

"He's a child. Life is less complicated for him."

"True. Tell me, were you tempted to run to me?"

"Only to look you in the eyes and ask how

you dared to come there when you'd snuck away without telling me goodbye."

He walked over, sat beside her and took her hand into his.

"Had I awakened you, I wouldn't have left." There. He'd said it. "Not your bed and perhaps not Chattanooga."

Her forehead crinkled. "I don't understand."

"I'm in love with you, Jenny." Saying the words out loud weakened his knees to jelly, left him vulnerable and feeling as if he should protect himself. Instead, he stared into Jenny's wide eyes and left his heart's fate in her hands.

"You love me?" Her voice trembled with disbelief.

Lifting her hand to his lips, he pressed a kiss there. "Madly. Passionately. Completely head-over-heels in love with you. I'm in unknown waters, Jenny. I've never known what it was to look at a person and to see my future, to be with them and to belong. My heart is yours."

Tristan loved her? Surely, Jenny's ears deceived her. Because what he was saying seemed impossible.

"I—I don't know what to say."

His hand holding hers shook. He sighed. "Say you'll give me another chance to prove I can be the man you and Sawyer need me to be."

"You want to take the travel nurse position in Chattanooga so you can be with Sawyer and me?"

He nodded. "Not a travel nurse position. I plan to get a permanent job with the hospital."

"Even if I say I don't want to see you?"

"If you say you don't want to see me, then my heart will be broken, but I won't give up because I know you care about me. I am going to return to Chattanooga and will earn your trust and your heart. Meeting you and Sawyer has given me something I've never had before."

She waited.

"A sense of home. Leaving has always been easy. Since I've been gone from here, my heart has ached to return. I never understood what it meant to come home, but from the moment I saw you at the airfield today, I knew."

"Chattanooga is home?"

"You're home, Jenny. You are my home."

"Because home is where the heart is?"

He lifted her hand to his lips again. "My heart

is with you and it's where the rest of me longs to be."

Everything he said sounded so wonderful, so like a dream, but fear clawed at the happiness she wanted to let fill her. "How do I know you won't leave again? How can I be sure?"

"You won't know, Jenny. Even I don't know what the future holds. All I've ever known is leaving one place after another, but not since I was a child have I wanted to stay somewhere. Then, I didn't have a choice but was at the mercy of those around me. Now, I have a choice, Jenny, and I choose you and Sawyer, if you'll have me."

What he was saying ran through her mind, jumbling as she tried to process what he meant. "You want to date me?"

He nodded. "I want everything with you, Jenny. To spend my life with you and Sawyer."

"He loves you so much."

Tristan cupped her face and stared into her eyes. "The question is, does his mother?"

"You know I do," she whispered back.

A smile spread across his face. "Then tell me."

"I love you, Tristan. With all my heart. That doesn't mean I'm not scared. Every man in my life has left me."

"I won't leave you, Jenny." He understood why she thought he would but, with clarity, he knew he wouldn't. "I'd rather die than hurt you and Sawyer. I'll finish out my contract in Chicago and when I come back to Chattanooga, I'm here to stay. My heart and my loyalty are yours as long as you want them."

Leaning toward him, she pressed her lips to his. "Then I want your heart, your loyalty, and all of you forever. Promise me."

Cupping her face, he stared into her eyes and he saw everything he hadn't known he'd wanted or needed reflected there. Without a doubt his next words were the easiest promise to keep that he'd ever made.

"I promise you my forever, Jenny."

And that was what he gave her. His heart. His love. His forever.

* * * * *